Journey Through
The White Night

By Dana Chandler

Journey Through the White Night

Dana Chandler

Copyright © 2025

Cover by Rachel Myers Media
rachelmyers.media@gmail.com

Human Created Symbol of Distinction

Published by KD Resources, a division of Digeology

ISBN 979-8-218-76717-4

Acknowledgement

To Emmalie Lee,

This book would not have been possible without you, my dear friend and travel companion. You were willing to take on an adventure to Alaska on a whim with courage, intelligence, and an unending and surprising sense of humor that I could not have endured without.

Be it your fear of earthquakes, your uncanny ability to get others to blurt out their life story, or your bravery with bears, thank you for not thinking me silly when I took copious notes in order to research the locations of this book. Your ideas with characters, settings, and plot lines were invaluable to this story.

From the bottom of my heart, I thank you.

Dana Chandler (right) with Emmalie Lee (left) on the
Mendenhall Glacier near Juneau, Alaska

Dedication

Brian, I miss you every day.

Brian Chandler

1963-2017

Prologue

He thought encrypting the email message would be more difficult than it was. All of those years spent with the Air Force learning codes and encryptions had paid off, even though he resented not being given a choice of jobs. He had wanted to be a pilot, but the Air Force had chosen another path for him.

"Everybody wants to be a pilot," His sergeant told him. "We need tech nerds."

Instead of being locked in a cock pit roaring at mock 1, he had been locked in a computer cubical analyzing code from our own military and breaking coded communications from other countries. He had become especially skilled with the Chinese codes. It was the Chinese codes, along with his top-secret clearance access to numerous communication systems, that had inspired him to create his own code.

Chapter 1

As Kate stepped out of the shower she thought of how fragile her body had become. How could age and use have taken such a toll? It seemed like it was just yesterday when she was kissing her first daughter off to school. The waves of big events flooded her memory; the girls' births, their first steps, their first day of school, their first boyfriends, graduations, weddings, the birth of her first grandchild…and then another. How life had slipped away from her. She wasn't "old" was she? After all, at the age of 57 there were still many more years ahead, but it was difficult to be hopeful about them. After toweling off and dressing she took her plastic tub full of nutritional supplements out from under the bathroom sink and took them into the kitchen where she put them on the table and carefully filled her two-week pill box. First, she counted the liquid calcium tablets, then the vitamin C, and so on until she had the breakfast cocktail of over-the-counter gems that her doctor had ordered her to take after giving her a diagnosis of osteoporosis.

"Whatever you do, don't break a bone. It will start a chain reaction that will be the end." She remembered her doctor saying recently, just before he listed off all of the "risky" activities that she could no longer participate in due to a possible fall.

Kate hadn't done many of the activities on the list for years, but somehow it seemed so final. Her life seemed over somehow. The finality of it all was overwhelming. She wished her husband, Matthew, were there to console her sense of loss, but thinking of him now only escalated her grief. There was no one to console her. What was she to do now? Sit in a rocking chair and just wither away? It felt like that was her only option.

Once the pill box was full, Kate went over to the computer to do a little research on osteoporosis treatments hoping to find a miracle article that would ease her mind concerning the crippling and painful time she feared was in front of her. As she was scrolling through a list of possible articles in her search engine, an ad popped up on the screen. "Alaska is Waiting-Escape Today!" was the heading, along with images of Mt. Denali (McKinley) and the Mendenhall Glacier near Juneau.

Chapter 2

Glancing out the window at the rain, Emma was glad she had chosen not to worry about getting to the yard work. Instead, she had decided to sort through her remaining boxes and totes from her move. She busied herself shredding useless documents and deciding what items she would keep and which ones she would donate to a local second-hand store.

Her pile of donations was getting fairly big, so she was going to go to the garage of her newly rented house to get an empty box when Danish, her German Dachshund, came wagging his tail as a sign that he had to go outside. Grabbing her jacket and her cell phone, Emma quickly opened the door. Danish hesitated because of the drizzle. He did not like the rain and liked using a wet lawn even less. His short legs always assured that he would not only have wet paws, but a wet belly as well. Emma coaxed him to the lawn.

"C'mon Danish."

The dog moved slowly, trying to stay under the rafter of the house to keep from getting wet. Emma giggled at the dog, remembering an old German Sheppard that her boys used to have that would cry when he got wet. Her boys were small at that time; ages 2, 6, and 12. Jeremy, her youngest would always want to pet the dog and hug it when it cried. While Daniel, her oldest, would grab its leash and try to drag it outside. The memory made her smile.

She thought of her boys now. All three married and with children. She wondered if her eight grandchildren enjoyed dogs as much as she did.

She recalled that she hadn't intended to get an animal in Germany. She remembered how Danish had come upon her porch one day with cuts and bruises on him. Without much effort, Emma had gained his friendship and then took him into her home and nursed him back to health. Though sheepish at first, the dog was loving and enjoyed snuggling up next to her on the couch. He was hesitant to take any table scraps from her, but finally took a piece of a Danish from her on the second day. It was easy after that to call him, "Danish." She shouldn't have named the dog, because that meant that somehow she had decided to keep him. She knew that she would have to find his owner. After five days she began asking around the military base where she worked if anyone knew who owned the dog.

Because all U.S. Department of Defense employees who live abroad must have their animals registered with the base they are assigned to, the owner was not difficult to identify. In finding the owner, she learned that they no longer wanted the dog and were looking for a new home for him. When he got out of their yard, they did not even attempt to find him in the hopes that the dog would not return. Emma learned that the dog was only a year old and had been kept in a kennel most of that time. He was ignored and treated badly when he was noticed.

She was glad she had offered to keep him. He had been great company and was well mannered most of the time.

Chapter 3

Yu Li was scared. She did not have experience with sneaking around and hiding things from her family. She had always tried to be a good daughter. She studied hard, worked hard, and never succumbed to her own pleasures, even when she would have been justified to do so. Now, however, she had no choice.

She worried about her mother. As the only daughter in her family, she knew it was her responsibility to care for her. After her father died she had taken that responsibility very seriously. She moved close to her mother, making sure that her needs were met before she even thought of herself. She and her mother both had jobs, but uneducated women were paid very little for their hours of toil each day in Shenzhen. Even with her ability to speak broken English, which landed her a front desk job at an electronic technology company, it was tough to get by.

When Dr. Wu had showed up at the office where she answered phones each day with an offer for her to take a package to someone in America, she should have known it wasn't a good idea to accept. But she needed the money as her expenses with her mother were adding up. The offer of 150,000 Yuan, if she delivered the item, would clear her debts and give them a cushion to live on.

She had taken the offer and quickly put the package that Dr. Wu had given her into her backpack. Within 24 hours she was given a visa to enter the US and a fake passport with her picture on it. Both forms of identification cleared customs and airport security, which sent her on a flight over the Pacific and on to Seattle.

Yu Li was wary. She knew deep in her gut that if she failed, things would be very bad for her and her mother. She must not fail.

Chapter 4

Kate had always wanted to travel through Alaska. At a younger age she had dreamt of trekking from Fairbanks to Anchorage along the railway with just her backpack. When she had mentioned that idea to Matthew, he was very encouraging and offered to go with her, as long as he could go see Denali. But the cancer took him before they could go.

She had always thought they would grow old together. She never expected either one of them to have health issues that would change all of that. Matthew's cancer was swift and final. It seemed that she didn't even get time to grasp the diagnosis before she was making end-of-life decisions for him. The memories of his tired and gaunt body had haunted her after he passed. As the years had gone, she could now remember him as the strong and virile man that he was before the cancer and it made her miss him even more.

Matthew was 6'2" with blondish gray hair when they met at the age of 45. Both of them had been through unhappy marriages and were not looking for another spouse. Their marriage was a spontaneous decision. Kate had just been offered a job in Asia with the U.S. Department of Defense. Matthew, being a former Navy submariner, knew that Kate would have to go alone unless they were wed. So, on a whim, with their children as their witnesses, they were married within 48 hours of Kate's job offer.

Although it was never perfect, Kate had no regrets about their marriage, except that she wished it had lasted longer. Kate smiled as she thought of how that quick decision had changed her life and given her a man who had loved her unconditionally.

Maybe another spontaneous decision would change her life again. She picked up the phone.

Chapter 5

The phone was ringing. Emma could hear it, but couldn't find where she had placed it. She frantically began digging in her jacket pocket and was able to put her finger on the screen before the connection stopped. She didn't take the time to see who was calling.

"Hello?"

"Emm, it's me, Kate."

"Oh, Hi!"

It had been a few months since they had last spoken. At that time, Emma had shared with Kate about her most recent move, coming back to the United States from Germany where she had lived for the past four years. She remembered how they had reminisced about their time together in Asia, where they were not only a good team at work, but dear friends after hours.

"How are you, Kate?"

"I'm okay."

Emma knew immediately that Kate had something on her mind. She had learned, after their years together in Japan and supporting her through Matthew's cancer, that Kate had a specific tone in her voice when things were troubling her.

"What is it?" Emma distinctively asked.

Kate hesitated. "Do you have a backpack?"

Emma knew Kate had already made some kind of plan and was just waiting for her to agree. "Yyyeeesss," she said slowly, hesitating to reply.

"Do you want to go to Alaska?"

"That's on my bucket-list!" Emma gleefully responded.

After the phone call had ended, Kate made arrangements for both women to go to Alaska for two weeks. Using only the internet, she booked flights, lodging, train reservations, ship reservations, and a rental car for a day in Juneau. In only three hours, the entire trip was planned and paid for before either woman could back out.

She made a list of all of the reservations and the cost and emailed it quickly to Emma. She then sent her a text that simply said, "We are all set for our journey through the white night!"

After the arrangements were all made, Kate wondered if she was making the right decision. She knew that Matthew had wanted to make this trip, though it felt empty to go without him. But she wanted to go on this trip too! Maybe it was time to make her own memories. She felt exhilarated and guilty all at the same time. Surely Matthew would be along and watching her from heaven as she traveled.

"You're over thinking this." She said to herself.

Maybe she was over thinking things. After all, it wasn't like she was changing careers and moving across the world. She grinned as she thought of the day that she and Matthew moved to Asia with only a few days to prepare.

She remembered leaving most of their possessions behind in the house that she had purchased in Washington State. The only thing Matthew wanted to take was his Harley Davidson Heritage motorcycle. He didn't care if he even took any clothes with him.

"Now that was an adventure!" She exclaimed as she looked upward as if talking to Matthew in heaven.

She half expected him to reply, and she could imagine his response about her trip in her head. He would have said, "You're crazy and I'm in." and then hugged her.

It made her smile. He would always go with her when she came up with some hair brained adventure for them to go on. But she had not planned adventures since Matthew died. Maybe that's what she was feeling bad about?

"It's time to live again." She stated firmly. "It starts today."

Chapter 6

Emma began rummaging through her moving boxes. She couldn't remember exactly which large box held her backpack and hiking gear. As she was opening the second box her phone rang again.

"What did you forget Kate?" she said to herself as she reached into her pocket for the phone.

A man's voice bellowed, "Hello Emm!"

She recognized him immediately. It was Jon, her first husband. While they were friendly and their divorce amiable, he usually didn't call unless he wanted something.

"Hi." Emma replied unenthusiastically.

"How are you doing?" he began.

Before she could respond, he continued, "I was wondering if you still had those music books that Jeremy used last year for his concert. He said that you probably still had them."

"I think I do, but most of my stuff is still in boxes."

"Well, I need them by tomorrow night."

Emma began to get irritated and then she had a thought. "I'll make you a deal." She said. "I promise that I'll open all my boxes and find the music books for you tonight, if you'll take Danish for a couple of weeks. I'm headed out of town and I need a dog sitter."

"Danish?" he sounded surprised. "Sure, but where are you going?"

"You could ask me where I was going when we were married, but we aren't anymore. Do we have a deal?"

"Sure, I love your dog. And maybe, you'll decide that we can get remarried when you get back." Jon said with a chuckle.

"I know you'll take good care of Danish. Thank you."

Emma hung up the phone and continued the undaunting task of opening her moving boxes. As luck would have it, the music books were in the first box she reached for.

"Alaska here I come!"

Chapter 7

Kate thought about the more rugged trip that she and Matthew had always talked about and was glad she had decided that she was too old to sleep on the ground. She had settled on unique vacation rentals or boarding houses instead of camping. She knew she was aging and feeling the anxiety of her recent diagnosis, because the 40-year-old Kate would have never missed a chance at sleeping under the stars using only a ground pad and a sleeping bag.

There was a part of her that was a little sad about missing a true nature experience. Maybe she was worried about breaking a bone or maybe grieving her youth, but she knew she would be miserable if she had chosen to camp instead of picking a bed to sleep in. She was also positive that Emma would not want to travel like that either.

Kate sent a group text to her daughters letting them know where she was going and then emailed them each the itinerary she had created. She immediately got a text back from her oldest child asking her why she was going to Alaska with a backpack.

"You must be losin' it mom." Another daughter texted in response.

Kate didn't try to explain and ignored the messages and turned her phone off.

Chapter 8

Emma began packing as soon as she found the music books. She was excited and eager to be ready for the days to come. As she was moving to the kitchen to grab her flashlight, she hit her shin on the corner of the wall.

"Ouch!" she said aloud.

In looking down, Emma could see a small amount of blood coming from a cut on her shin. She went to the bathroom, gathered what first-aid supplies she could find and sat on the edge of the bathtub to bandage her leg. It hurt and it had taken her awhile to find the bandages and dress the wound. She would just go to bed and finish packing in the morning.

Emma lay in bed that night with great anticipation. Because she had been distracted by her wound, she realized that she'd forgotten her evening ritual of checking the earthquakes worldwide. She sat up in bed to check her phone. As she checked the typical website for the daily earthquake report with the National Geological Society, she immediately noticed the word "Alaska" on the most recent quake activity. A small quake, measuring 4.0 on the Richter Scale had just occurred off the coast of Sutwik Island. Now some of her anticipation was turning to anxiety as she worried about the possibility of an earthquake in the Aleutians while they were there.

Emma's mind wandered. She struggled to remember exactly where she was. Her mind moved between the present and Japan in 2011. She had been at school when it happened. At 2:46pm on a Friday afternoon as the high school students were in the halls getting ready to go home for the weekend, it began. It started slow at first, but quickly began to jerk the building and floor sideways. Emma heard the principal of the school yell at the students, "Get out! Get out!" Emma turned to her and yelled, "get under the table!" as she quickly dove under the table in her office and hung onto the leg of the table. Emma was there, under the table...alone.

It was tough to know if this was a memory or if it was happening again, but there was not a table in this little bedroom so it must just be in her memory.

Emma lost all memory of those minutes when the earthquake jolted and jarred her office. It was as though her mind blocked the memory of falling objects, people yelling, and the crashing noises. When she became conscience of her surroundings again, it was eerily quiet. The halls were still and there was no one in them. As Emma rose from under the table, she was aware that the ground was still shaking...silently. She made her way down the hall. She had to hold the walls to stay upright. It reminded her of the Tom Sawyer Island swinging bridge in Disneyland that she had once walked over.

Before reaching the door of the school, another teacher came by her. "This has gone on for 15 minutes now!" the teacher exclaimed while looking at his watch. "When is it going to stop?"

Emma did not respond. She knew she needed to get out of the building.

Once she made it out of the front door of the school, she retreated to the parking lot. Car alarms were going off, as the cars had been shaken enough in the quake that their sensors had signified a security alert. Other people had gathered there as well.

The principal of the school spotted her and ran to her and gave her a big hug. "I didn't know if you were okay. You stayed in the building a long time. I'm glad you're out now."

Emma still struggled to speak. She knew she was in shock, but wasn't sure what she could do about it. She was physically trembling...or was that just the ground shaking. She noticed the power poles were moving back and forth with the powerlines coming very close to the building, the cars, and those in the parking lot. "Are the power poles going to fall?" She asked quietly. No one heard her.

Emma noticed that the principal was talking to those in the parking lot, trying to get a sense of who was still on campus when the earthquake hit. Some of the high schoolers living on base that had run home, were starting to come back now because they didn't know what to do and there were no adults at home to guide them. Emma watched the principal taping notes on the front door of the building, letting people know who was accounted for and where they were. Emma was making mental notes, and was amazed at the ingenuity of it, but outwardly seemed frozen and unable to help.

The principal noticed Emma standing in the parking lot, frozen, non-verbal, and unable to help. "Go home." She said to Emma. "I'll take care of things here."

Without even realizing it, Emma turned and walked to her car in the parking lot. She pulled out her keys from her pocket and started the car. "Now what?" she thought, as her mind returned to the present.

Now she had second thoughts about going to Alaska.

"No." she thought to herself. "I'm not letting fear stop me."

She put her phone on the night stand and rolled over in bed.

Chapter 9

After she was done packing, Kate confirmed all of the reservations she had made. Because she knew that there were some places that they were going that did not have WIFI, she printed copies and then slid them into the back pocket of her backpack.

She then went into her sewing room and made six face masks for the trip. With the COVID 19 requirements, they would be required to wear masks whenever they were indoors. The pandemic had been ravaging the world for at least 16 months now and vaccines had helped to remedy the long-term impacts, but not until millions had died. Kate did not want to ruin their trip by getting the illness. She'd had the Delta variant several months ago and was so sick that four days had passed before she realized it.

"Three masks each should be enough for us," she thought. "We can wear one during the day and wash them out each evening."

Kate then loaded the car with her things to begin the eight-hour drive to Emma's house. She texted Emma to let her know she was on her way and pulled out of the driveway.

Chapter 10

Emma put the music books she had found the day before, Danish's leash and kennel, along with a supply of dog food in the car. Then she talked Danish into getting in and they made the 50-mile drive to Jon's house. Though Jon wanted to visit, Emma gave him the books, unloaded the kennel and dog food, gave Danish a big squeeze, and got back in the car.

Emma lowered her window. "Be a good boy..." she said as she drove away, "both of you!"

Jon was laughing as they waved good bye.

Emma giggled too and enjoyed the brief encounter. She thought about how much fun Jon had been during the early years of their marriage. Oh, how she wished their relationship could have stayed that way. Oh well. She couldn't control what had happened to them then, and she sure wasn't going to cry over it now. The marriage had been over for years and she was just glad that they were able to remain friends for their boys' sake.

Chapter 11

The email response confirmed the meeting time and place. He knew no one would track his email with the unique encoding he used because he had developed it himself while serving at Elmendorf.

***

Elmendorf was not the base that he had wanted to be stationed. He had aspirations of being a fighter pilot, but that was not to be. With his career-imposed specialty in cyber operations, he had been assigned in the northern regions to keep an eye on Asia and Russia. This had worked to his advantage now. He was a gifted code breaker and hacker…and he knew it.

His emotions flared as he thought about Colonel Simpson who was always telling him to control his temper.

"If you would talk reasonably to people instead of yell at them, you might get something done." The colonel had said to him one day after he'd had a disagreement with another colleague.

"Well, if he hadn't been so stupid, then I wouldn't have needed to yell at him." He remembered responding.

At that, Colonel Simpson ordered him out of the lab. That infuriated him. The colonel was taking sides, and it wasn't his.

"Why?" he screamed, as he flailed his arms over the desk and cleared everything off of it. His keyboard flew across the room and his computer fell to the floor.

It made him angrier every time he thought of the incident. He was justified in his response. No one else would do anything about the colleague, who couldn't code to save his life. As he saw it, Colonel Simpson, and those other weak officers, couldn't do anything right and took too long to make decisions…except the decision to demote him for simply giving his opinion.

The United States Air Force had treated him like dirt, so he would treat them the same way, and make it hurt.

He didn't know who was responding to his email, but he did know that they were probably not going to be the person who met him. He only knew that the person he was to meet would be wearing a royal blue baseball cap with a peace sign on it and a backpack.

Chapter 12

Kate arrived at Emma's just as Emma was clipping her backpack closed.

"Perfect timing!" Emma said as she greeted her friend.

Emma put her backpack in the back of Kate's car and the two friends began their adventure to the land of the midnight sun.

Chapter 13

The email came through the security system like hundreds of others that were flagged for security screening. This email however, used a rare coding system to prevent the security officer from reading it. "What is this?" Staff Sergeant Jall said as she tried to decipher the email. She couldn't decode it, but she knew it needed further inspection because the encoding was so tough to translate. She quickly called her commander and sent the email electronically to him.

"I haven't been able to break the security coding." Staff Sergeant Jall explained.

Colonel Brian Johnson clicked into the file he was sent and his mouth dropped open. "Deem this email top secret, staff sergeant. No questions...just do it."

"Yes, sir." She responded.

Once off of the phone, the commander sent a text, "White Night"

He quickly got a response, "Drill?"

"REAL TIME...not exercise"

"Received and Confirmed"

Chapter 14

The excitement in the car was like giddy school girls getting ready for their first school dance. While the laughter certainly dominated the conversation, at one point Emma voiced her concerns about the geologic occurrences recently along the Aleutian Islands.

"We've already been through one of the largest earthquakes on record, Kate, and I DO NOT want to go through that again."

"Don't worry Emm. I bought insurance in case of a natural disaster. The insurance company will fly us out of there if something happens. We know what to do. Besides, the chances are pretty slim." Kate responded with a giggle.

"I'm serious." Emma retorted. "I have so much PTSD from the last one I don't think I could survive another one emotionally."

"I get it, Emm. But I'm sure it will be fine."

"Promise me?" Emma pleaded.

"I promise!" Kate assured her. "Now let's go have some fun!"

They arrived in Seattle late in the evening. They found their hotel and asked about where they could park their car while they were gone, before calling it a night.

Chapter 15

He arrived early and ordered a burger and sat back in the food court at the White Center Mall near Seattle. He surveyed his surroundings, noticing some of the other patrons at the food court and looking for someone with a royal blue baseball cap with a peace sign on it.

He was cautious. Besides wearing his blue Mariners baseball hat deep over his brow, he didn't want to look suspicious so he would sometimes look down and pick at his meal, although he didn't think he could actually taste what he was eating. He made a sweeping glance to look for anyone who looked out of place or if there was anyone in his peripheral who was watching him. He visually scanned for security cameras that might give him away, but all that he could see were at a far enough distance that his face would not be recognizable. His surroundings appeared to be safe and he was pleased that his contact had chosen this public place.

After about 20 minutes, right at the arranged time, a young Chinese woman wearing a royal blue baseball hat with a peace sign stepped into the Subway order line. She had a small backpack on her back and looked around cautiously. She didn't look like a veteran at this. She looked far too young and acted nervous.

"I'd better do this quickly before she bails." He thought to himself as he stood and moved toward the Subway counter. He took the item out of his pocket as he reached her. He knew it couldn't be a direct meeting, so while she was waiting in the line, he bumped into her and then dropped the object out of his hand.

She understood and pretended to be knocked off balance enough to drop her backpack. He picked up her backpack, slid out a small package from the side pocket into his hand, and said a silent, "pardon me" before he walked away. She quickly picked up her backpack and the memory stick that had been dropped and stood back up in the line.

Chapter 16

Yu Li was terrified. She wanted to get rid of the memory stick she had just been given as soon as possible. She immediately stepped from the fastfood line and left the mall, heading toward the hotel to meet Dr. Wu and give him the stick.

Once she arrived at the hotel where she was to meet Dr. Wu, she found that no one was there. There was a piece of paper on the bed that simply said, "Anchorage" with a printed flight boarding pass with her name paperclipped to the note.

Yu Li was confused. She was instructed not to carry anything on her person for long. She would have to get to Anchorage with the memory stick on her. This was getting more dangerous and much more than she had bargained for.

Chapter 17

In the morning, Kate and Emma went to the new Daiso Store that had recently opened in South Seattle.

"I absolutely LOVE the Daiso!" Emma exclaimed as the two of them wandered down the isle of the Japanese store.

"It reminds me so much of our time in Japan. I miss it so much." Kate joined in.

Both women bought items either for the trip or for their grandchildren before heading back to the hotel.

"Pack what you need and we'll leave the rest in the car for when we get back." Kate said.

"That was so much fun!" Emma said to her friend.

"Just wait until we get to the abbey!" Kate responded as she reminded Emma that she had reserved an old abbey as their accommodations while they were in Fairbanks.

***

After a shuttle to the airport and a trip through TSA Security, they hurried to their gate for their flight. Once inside the airport terminal the seriousness of the recent pandemic was obvious. Everyone was required to wear a mask, as well as stay six feet away from each other if they were not traveling together. In some ways the airport seemed like a Sci Fi film. Not many people had dared to go out since the global disease totally shutdown most businesses months earlier, but the ones who did venture out seemed to be cautious.

It made Kate think of the zombie movies she had seen where everyone was afraid that the person next to them was a zombie and somehow, they might catch it.

Kate took it seriously though. She had volunteered in the early days of the shutdown to make masks and personal protective equipment (PPE) for her niece who was a doctor at a local hospital. The hospital couldn't get any PPE. The demand was so great that all of the suppliers were out of gowns, masks, and gloves.

Kate and her sisters had sewn two full protective outfits for her niece. Once her niece wore them to work, everyone at the hospital wanted one. Kate and her sisters had made dozens of gowns and hundreds of masks for people. She wondered if the world would ever be able to move past this pandemic. It worried her and she mentioned it to Emma.

"The world will go back to normal again, but it will be a while." Emma reassured her friend.

"Maybe we should have waited until some of this passed?" Kate asked.

"Well, it's a little late now." Emma quipped sarcastically.

They both chuckled a little.

"I suppose it is." Kate said softly. "You're worried about an earthquake and I'm worried about catching something."

"I guess we will both have to face our fears."

"I guess we will." Kate said as she grabbed Emma's hand and squeezed. "We're in this together."

Chapter 18

Agents James "Jim" Robertson and Herman Schmit sat in the command center at Elmendorf's security center while they were briefed on the email that had come through with the unique coding system created by an especially talented technician who had an exceptional understanding of code and learned skills quickly.

Their suspicions about the coder were based on the technician's record. He had joined the Air Force right out of high school in order to make a name for himself and show his father that he was better than the rest of the family. This technician was cocky and smart, but had difficulty getting along with others and controlling his temper. He was demoted several times for insubordination and eventually dismissed from duty for unbecoming behavior after he got angry at his superior officer and threw his computer.

After his dismissal, the technician had made several threats to his commanders and with a little investigation, agent Jim Robertson also had found a credible communication the technician had sent to the Chinese government offering top secret information about a United States satellite weaponry system that was being tested over the Central Alaskan Mountain Range.

Jim and Herman both recognized the rendering in the email communication immediately and knew it must mean that Chinese espionage was currently at play.

Neither man was surprised. There is a new incident report regarding spying by the Chinese every twelve hours on average in the United States. However, this particular case was unnerving because of the unique coding used to encrypt the email. That meant that the perpetrator they were looking for was known by them and a former United States airman. This could mean that he would be easier to find or harder to find if the Chinese got to him first.

Jim and Herman knew the suspected infiltrator had made some kind of exchange in the Seattle area and then booked a flight to Fairbanks. What exactly he planned on doing there, was still unknown, but they needed to find out.

Herman made a call and the two headed for a small airfield toward Wasilla. They could be in Fairbanks in a couple of hours if all went well.

Chapter 19

The Fairbanks airport was small, but quaint. There was a large taxidermy polar bear in a glass case in the middle of the only lobby and terminal. Hanging from the ceiling was a small bush plane, an example of what was used to transport people and supplies to the far-off regions of the tundra. Kate's and Emma's arrival in the late evening was uneventful until it came time to leave the airport. There were no shuttles to reserve so Kate had assumed they could get a taxi from the airport to the abbey where she had arranged for them to stay for the night. However, a taxi was tough to find.

"There must be only three taxis in all of Fairbanks." Emma joked as they waited outside the airport doors for a taxi...or any traffic at all.

Kate called a number for a taxi and soon found out that Emma was fairly close to correct. They waited about an hour and a half, but eventually a taxi did come for them.

The taxi driver was talkative. He was curious where the women were from and why they wanted to come to Fairbanks.

"How did you end up here in Alaska?" Emma asked him.

The driver sat back, took a deep breath, and shared his story. He was from the Midwest of the United States. He was engaged to be married. All was going well until one day he had an anxiety attack because he was settling for a life that he didn't want. He had an argument with his fiancé about his misgivings. When the argument didn't go well, he told his fiancé that he was going fishing.

"Was she mad that you went fishing?" Kate asked.

"I don't know. I never went back. I've been here ever since."

A little shocked, Kate asked, "How long ago was that?"

"About fifteen years now." The taxi driver laughed with a deep roaring laugh. So did both Emma and Kate.

***

When they arrived at the abbey, the taxi driver explained that he would go into the abbey with them because he'd never delivered anyone to this particular place and wanted to make sure the women were taken care of before he left them. Kate and Emma appreciated his care.

Once inside, it was discovered that the place was in fact the abbey, but that the guest quarters were in what was called the "abbey annex," which was a half mile away. Emma and Kate were so grateful the taxi driver had stayed with them.

They quickly loaded back into the cab and drove to the annex of the abbey. It was abandoned. Aside from their taxi in the driveway, the place was lifeless. The abbey's annex appeared to be a small old apartment building that was being renovated. The concert beams were showing and the outside was only half covered with siding. The other half was bare to the support beams. There were piles of renovation rubbish, such as busted up concrete, sheet rock, and old furniture on two sides of the building.

"Well, I guess we'll have privacy." Emma mused.

"I'm so sorry Emm. This looked much better online." Kate said as she looked around at the construction piles near the building.

"Well, the only thing you'll have to worry about out here are the bears." The driver added. "Now, let's get you inside."

Kate used the key given to her by the woman at the abbey and opened the door. It opened to a hallway with two doors in it; one to the right and one at the end of the hall. Kate looked at the key and turned to the door on the right.

Once inside the doorway, the taxi driver assured them that either he or his colleague would be back to get them in the morning and then left. The two friends looked around the room. There were two beds in the apartment, along with two couches, two big chairs, a dining sized table with chairs, refrigerator, electric stove, and an assortment of night stands.

"This looks like the room they store the furniture in." Kate said sarcastically.

"Well, let's hope it's clean." Emma responded.

As Emma sat down to decide where to store her things, she felt fluid wash over her lower leg. Examining it, she saw that her pant leg was wet. As she pulled up her pant leg, puss ran down the front of her shin from the wound she had gotten a couple days earlier. It was red and swollen. The gash had widened and yellow green fluid was running from the middle.

"Kate, I think we'll have to take a detour."

"What do you mean?" Kate asked.

Emma showed her the wound and both agreed that she needed to see a doctor right away. It was obvious that the wound was infected and neither of them had any antibiotics with them.

Kate called the taxi company's phone number again. The person answering said that they could be there within the hour.

The next taxi driver spoke with a Filipino accent. He was polite and quiet. When Emma asked him to take them to the nearest urgent care clinic, he let them know that there was not an urgent care clinic in Fairbanks that was open that late at night. Knowing that they had to be at the train station by 8:30am the next morning, Emma asked the driver to take them to the hospital.

Once at the hospital, the driver told Kate, "Call the number when the exam is over and me or my friends will take you back to your room." He nodded toward the door and continued, "Wear your mask in there. We have sickness everywhere here."

Kate thanked him and both women put on their masks and Kate followed Emma into the Emergency Room.

The hospital was busy! There were sick and coughing people everywhere. Emma approached the counter warily without touching it. She explained that she had a wound that she believed was infected. After being asked if she had tested positive for any respiratory diseases in the last 14 days, the attendant asked her to wait. Emma and Kate did not remove their masks and found a corner near the door to stand in while waiting for a doctor.

Emma was taken back into an inner room, leaving Kate in the waiting room. Because the room was full of sick people, Kate stepped out the door and decided to wait outside where the air more easily circulated. She did not want to get sick on the trip. She hoped that Emma was not getting exposed in a back room.

It was after 10pm, but the sun still hung on the horizon. Several people went in and out of the Emergency Room door. Kate overheard many conversations. One native woman came out with two children, both of whom had very runny noses and coughs. She was complaining because she had a friend that had recently died from the epidemic and the doctors were refusing to help her children. Kate felt sorry for her, but did not approach her. Soon a young native man with his dog in the cab of a worn out pickup truck came and picked her up. He would not allow her to sit in front of the truck with his dog. Even though it was late and chilly, he made the woman and the two children sit in the bed of the truck before driving off.

Kate thought about how lucky she was. This woman obviously was treated poorly by others. She didn't fight it, she just accepted it, and tolerated it. This made Kate sad. Matthew had always treated her with respect and would never have expected her to sit in the back, particularly with two sick little kids. She had been truly blessed.

In one of the back rooms of the hospital, Emma was attended by a very handsome young male doctor. He confirmed that Emma's leg was, in fact, infected. The labs had revealed that it was a simple infection which should clear up in a few days after a bout of antibiotics. He explained to Emma that the COVID 19 outbreak was rampant in Fairbanks and had hit the native Eskimo population hard. There had been many deaths, but there was no treatment that had proven very effective yet and the natives didn't trust the government's vaccines. Because he didn't want Emma to have to go to a pharmacy and risk more exposure, he gave her two weeks' worth of oral pills and told her to take one twice a day until they were gone. Then he advised that Emma leave Fairbanks right away. When Emma explained that she and her friend were due on the morning train to Denali, he seemed relieved and wished her safe travels.

When Emma left the back room, she held her mask tight over her face and walked straight out the door, hoping Kate would be there to greet her. Kate called the taxi again and the two waited in front of the hospital.

They were silent at first as they waited, but then Emma shared with Kate what the doctor had told her.

"I guess being isolated out in that old abbey annex isn't so bad then." Kate said.

"I'm thinking it was a blessing in disguise." Emma told her as the taxi pulled up to the curb.

It was close to midnight before they reached the abbey annex. The sky was darkening, but not completely, as the northern night only had about an hour of dusk-like darkness in the summer. The two women had been going full steam for a couple of days. Both were tired and hungry. They each chose a bed and slept.

After a good night's sleep they were both ready to go and waiting in the driveway at 8am for the taxi. The morning driver was a couple of minutes late.

"Good morning" the man said with a Russian accent.

"Thank you for coming." Kate said. "We have to be at the train by 8:30."

"Not a problem. I will get you there on time." He said.

The taxi driver was kind and full of joy. Emma asked where he was from and he said that he was from Moscow, Russia. Emma asked him how he had come to Alaska and he told the story of oppression in Russia and his desire to have his wife and children live free in America. He said that they had to apply for a visa, which took a couple of years, but once they got to the states they made a plan to never leave. He was offered a job logging near Fairbanks, which is what had brought the family here. But then later, was offered a job as a taxi driver, so he took it. His wife was a cook at a local restaurant and his children both had graduated from high school at the local school. He said that he loved Alaska and would never leave.

Emma and Kate both liked him. He was kind and obviously admired his family and treated his passengers well.

Emma shared with him that she had lived in Moscow and worked there for the United States Consulate. The driver stopped talking almost instantly and seemed to be suspicious of the two women.

"Why are you here in Fairbanks?" he asked them.

Oblivious to his change in behavior, Kate began to explain about their train trip. Emma however, noticed his change right away. She added that they were just tourists and that she no longer worked for the US government, nor had any contact with anyone in Russia.

This seemed to settle the man's anxiety a little and he was more willing to converse with the women after that, but did not share anything more about himself. When they arrived at the train station, the taxi driver took their backpacks to the check-in area, set them down on a bench, and bid them a good day.

"Did you notice how nervous he got when I mentioned what I did in Moscow?" Emma asked Kate.

"Yes, a little, but I'm not sure why he would be nervous around us." Kate responded.

"I think he was worried that I was spying on him. The Russian government does follow people, even out of the country."

"Poor man." Kate said empathetically. "His secrets are safe with us."

"I just want to know if anyone here is actually from Alaska." Emma quipped.

Chapter 20

With his Mariners cap pulled down close to his eyes he deboarded the plane and went to the cue line for a taxi. As he waited for what seemed like hours, he called a hotel and reserved a room. By the time a taxi finally came he was on edge and irritated. He thought he would have more time in Fairbanks. The Alaska Tours office was closed for the night so he couldn't reserve the ticket he needed on the train. He would have to do it in the morning.

He rose early and took the hotel shuttle to the train station. A family of three had just cancelled their tickets at the last minute so he was able to book a seat on the Denali Star. He marveled at his streak of good luck.

He didn't notice the two men who had cued up in the ticket line behind him, purchasing the last two remaining tickets.

It was time now to plan for how he would get his belongings through the Alaskan tundra without detection. He went to the coffee counter and ordered a latte. As he looked at the crowd awaiting the Denali Star for boarding, he noticed a backpack sitting on a bench next to a woman with white hair. He made a mental note of her backpack with the Navy emblem. He neared the backpack without the woman noticing. When her back was turned, he quickly slipped the small package into the side pocket and then stepped back to watch the woman.

She was traveling with a woman companion. The two seemed to be good friends as they were talking and laughing with each other. They cued quickly in the line of passengers headed for the Denali Star. He knew he could not lose sight of them.

Chapter 21

Kate and Emma cued through the line, gave their large backpacks to the luggage attendant and waited for the train to board. Once it was time, each person in the group of passengers walked along the tracks until they came to the car number on their ticket. Emma and Kate were assigned in the last car of the Denali Star Line, which they considered to be the best seats on the entire train. They had paid extra to have the window ceiling so that they could take advantage of the views.

After masking up and going up a set of spiral stairs, they found their seats toward the front of the car. Their car was assigned a personal tour guide named, Dan, who welcomed them and then told them to make themselves comfortable and get acquainted with their surroundings.

The train car was exceptionally designed. Upstairs, the passengers enjoyed beautiful seating with a 180° view and a drink bar at the front of the car. At the back of the car was a spiral stairwell that led to the lower level where there were two glamorously decorated bathrooms; one on either side of the isle, and the dining facilities. At the front of the dining facilities was a small kitchen. In the rear of the dining facilities, past the bathrooms, was a small balcony where passengers could stand outside to view the surroundings. Emma and Kate were amazed at how efficiently the design of the car was laid out, making sure that passengers had everything that they needed without leaving the car.

"Now this is traveling in luxury!" Emma exclaimed as they found their seats.

"And our kids think we're hiking around with a backpack and sleeping in a tent fighting off bears." Both women laughed together.

"Let them think that." Emma said, "We are tough old broads."

***

The landscape leaving Fairbanks was flat and sometimes forest laden. Kate was surprised that it wasn't mostly pine trees like she had expected. Instead, the timberland was a variety of trees from aspen to pine to birch. The birch trees were particularly beautiful with their white bark and nubby knots. Kate loved the fresh smell and began to feel a little lighter in her spirit. She missed Matthew, but knew that he was there with her. She could feel him. And though she was glad at how close she felt to him at that moment, as they distanced themselves from Fairbanks, she somehow felt sadness as if she would have to let him go somewhere along the way.

Emma gazed over the forested tundra and was reminded of her time in Russia. The landscape was similar and it brought back memories of picnics with her youngest son, as she single parented behind the iron curtain. The security was everywhere there. There were many days that Emma knew the KGB had been in their apartment during the day when she and Jeremy were gone. They were constantly under surveillance and sometimes she would make jokes about how many times the security cameras had caught her using the bathroom.

There typically was not heat control. The government decided when the heat would be turned on, so there were cold nights and little control of everyday happenings.

But there were good memories in Moscow too. She and Jeremy would go on picnics in the park near their old Soviet cement block apartment. She loved watching him explore his world. At the time, he wasn't yet old enough for school and still had that preschool curiosity in him. He loved the trees and would pretend that they were his imaginary friends.

Emma loved meeting the local Russians who would then introduce her to more of their friends. She loved that most people were good, even if she didn't like the politics in their country. The Russians were quirky, like producing the cat circus and the marionette shows for adults. But she loved the food and she loved the subway.

She smiled at the memories.

As the train progressed, the rolling prairie transformed into steep valleys meandering along a marshy river and creek beds with mountainous terrain. Kate wandered down to the balcony at the back of the train. The weather was beautifully sunny with a few wisps of clouds. The air was slightly nippy, but felt fresh and crisp. Traveling along a meadow near a river bank, a moose walked along the train tracks seemingly nodding hello to the train. Kate knew Matthew was there with her.

As a history buff, Emma was intrigued about the history of the path they were following. She noticed some square poles along the railway. Dan, the tour guide, explained that the square poles with the glass transformer blocks were the original telegraph poles, from the early twentieth century, connecting Anchorage with Fairbanks. The poles had continuous wire between stations and messages were sent along sections of the line in order for communication to continue even when the path was not passable by humans. Even though the line had been abandoned decades ago with the dawn of the telephone, most of the lines were still standing today.

As the train pulled across the Tanana River near Nenana, Dan shared many stories with the passengers. He shared about President Harding hammering in the last spike of the railway connecting the towns of the Pacific coast to the inner Alaskan tundra in Nenana in 1923.

And the wonderful story of the dog Balto, who, in 1933, along with his team of dogs and musher Leonhard Seppala, took much needed medicine by dog sled from Nenana, up to the diphtheria ridden citizens of Nome.

And the story of when the locals in Nenana all lined up near the train tracks to greet it with their line of mooning butts as a protest because they were unhappy with a politician that was riding on the train.

These little stories were very interesting and entertaining to Emma. Kate loved them too.

Because Dan used a microphone, they could wander around the car and still hear his tales. Needing to use the bathroom, Kate walked to the back of the car and down the spiral stairs. The restrooms were both being occupied so she waited at the lower back of the car. As she looked out over the back balcony, she could imagine a line of 20 people turning their backsides toward the train and ripping down their pants to moon the passengers. She laughed aloud at the thought.

A deep chuckle came from behind her. Surprised, she looked over her shoulder at a man with enchanting brown eyes. Even though he had his mask on, she could tell he was smiling because of the wrinkles around his eyes.

"What's tickled your fancy?" he asked amused.

Thankful that her blushed face was mostly covered by her mask, she said, "I was just thinking about all those people who mooned the train."

"That was pretty funny. I suppose that's the Alaskan way to protest." He chuckled a little more. They both did.

Just then the bathroom door opened and Kate went in. After she had gone to the bathroom washed her hands, and made sure that her mask was secure, she joined Emma in the upper car. She couldn't help think about the mysterious man at the bathroom.

Chapter 22

The landscape became even more rugged as the train wound its way through the Alaska Range southward toward Denali National Park. The steep river gorge showed signs of recent landslides and rock fall. The train tracks were nestled so close to the canyon wall that Emma thought she could reach out and touch the mountain.

Dan began to speak on the microphone, "We will soon be slowing down. We need to go through an old tunnel. Please listen carefully to the engineer's announcement."

Wondering what was happening, the passengers in the train quieted. The train began slowing down until it was at a complete stop. Emma and Kate could see that there was indeed a tunnel opening ahead, but the train stopped before entering.

After several moments, the intercom sounded, "Hello everyone, this is Reginald Gordan, the engineer of the Denali Star. We will be entering a tunnel just before we arrive in Denali township. This tunnel, at times, is susceptible to cave-ins and landslides so we will be waiting for an "all clear" from our spotters. Once we are in the tunnel, we will be moving slowly as not to disturb anymore of the fragile schist then necessary.

"Oh, that doesn't sound good. They have earthquakes here too, you know." Emma said.

As the train began to inch forward Emma and Kate could see the front of the train enter the tunnel as it curved into the mountain.

"I wonder if it's really dangerous or if this is just an added drama for tourists." Kate rationalized.

Whether it was drama or not, as they entered the tunnel both women could see the large rocks along the tracks that had fallen from the ceiling of the tunnel. Small drips of water wept down the walls. There were wooden beams about every 10 feet to stabilize the soil around them. As they moved deeper into the tunnel the light grew scarce and they could no longer see around them. Water continued to run onto the glass roof above them and occasionally a small rock would fall as well.

"I don't think this is for drama. This would not be a good spot to get caught in an earthquake." Emma responded.

"We aren't going to have an earthquake, Emma." Kate reassured.

Both were relieved to see the light emerge on the other side of the tunnel.

The valley suddenly widened and they could see the townsite of Denali which began on the valley floor and climbed up the sides. The train depot was a cute little building made of logs. It looked small, but once off of the train, the women could see that there were several buses parked on paved areas along the edge of the mountain moving up in elevation from the station.

Drivers were standing with signs that showed the accommodations they represented. Kate found the man holding the "Denali Bluffs

Hotel" sign and motioned for Emma to follow her. Both women loaded their backpacks into the storage area of the bus and climbed aboard. Once on the bus, they found a double seat near the front. Kate put her day pack at her feet and pulled out her phone to look at her map app.

"Well, hello." Came a familiar voice.

Kate looked up to see the enchanting brown eyes she had seen near the bathroom earlier.

"Hello." She responded. Not knowing what else to say, she looked back down at her map app hoping he would move past her. She felt her face go flush as the man moved past.

"Who was that?" Emma asked in surprise.

"I don't know. I just ran into him at the bathroom earlier on the train."

"Please tell me you at least got his name!" Emma said.

"Well…no." Kate sighed. "Why would I do that?"

"C'mon Kate. Anybody could see he's an attractive man and giving you signs that he's interested."

"Interested in what?"

Emma hit her friend gently on the arm. "You're not dead Kate." She said sarcastically. "Matthew would say it's okay for you to move on."

Kate was silent. Her thoughts raced. She hadn't thought about getting a man in her life since Matthew. How could she ever find a man like him again. Somehow it would feel like a betrayal of what they had together. And yet, she did like being swooned over. Something about a man's attention made her feel like she mattered. She had assumed that would never happen again once Matthew was gone.

The bus ride to the Denali Bluffs was beautiful and steep. They crossed the valley and went over the river to the little townsite of Denali before beginning the narrow steep climb to the hotel. Once at the hotel Emma and Kate disembarked the bus and went to the storage area for their packs. Kate grabbed hers quickly and went into the hotel hoping to avoid the brown eyed man.

"You're being silly Kate." Emma prodded.

Chapter 23

When the train arrived at Denali townsite, he had watched the women as they made their way to the bus for the "Denali Bluffs Hotel." He quickly followed and boarded the same bus. He walked past the women, making sure he did not draw their attention. They were deep in conversation and did not seem to notice him. Once at the hotel, he cued up behind them at the registration desk and heard the clerk say, "Room 346" as he handed them an electronic lock keycard. Now he knew where they were staying.

"Can we have lunches prepared for our tour into the park tomorrow?" one of the women asked.

"Sure," the hotel desk clerk said. "Which tour are you on?"

"We are on the 9am bus." She replied.

As soon as the women exited the lobby he went to the registration desk and booked a single suite for two nights.

"Is there a tour going into the park tomorrow that I can get on?" he asked the clerk.

"There is one left with seats. It's the late bus and leaves at 9am. Is that okay?"

"That's perfect." He said.

Chapter 24

The two women found their way to their room overlooking the vast valley. The room faced Denali National Park with views of high peaks and the forested valley laid out like a painting. They were directly above the townsite, so could only see a few buildings on the far side of the valley.

"This is beautiful!" Kate exclaimed as she opened the curtains to view the scene. The entire wall was windows so the view was as far as you could see to the left and the right.

"Amazing!" Emma exclaimed.

Only after gazing at the spectacular view for a while did the women look at the rest of the room. It was quaintly decorated as a mountain cabin with wildlife photos on the walls and high wooden beams on the ceiling. The quilts on the two beds matched, sewn in a wood-colored theme, with log nightstands. It was calming and lovely.

After the women put their things down in the room, they decided to explore the townsite of Denali. It was late afternoon and there were rain clouds above the steep peaks in the distance. They grabbed their raincoats and headed down the hill from the hotel.

The town of Denali was built of small log buildings with a wooden walkway most of the length of town. There were souvenirs shops, a few restaurants, and a couple of office shops where tourists could arrange for adventure excursions. The town was filled with people.

Kate and Emma masked when they entered each shop, but mostly walked absent mindedly as they ventured along the boardwalk.

"I'm getting hungry." Kate mentioned as they were leaving one shop. "Let's find somewhere to have dinner."

Now outside and freeing themselves from their masks, Emma agreed. With Kate in the lead, they both left the wooden boardwalk to go to the restaurants on the uphill side of town. As Emma was stepping off of the last step of the boardwalk, she slipped and began to fall. She felt a strong arm slip around her waist and steady her.

"Here, let me help you, little lady." She heard a man say in a deep smooth voice.

She looked up into a face etched with years of experience that she hoped he would share with her.

Chapter 25

Once he knew the women were far enough down the hill that they could not see back to their room, he made his way to their door. Using his electronic code hacking system, he unlocked the door, stepped in quickly, and closed the door again. He did not want to stay in the room any longer than necessary. He spotted the backpack with the Navy emblem right away. He unzipped the outside side pocket and removed the small package. He opened it and took one of the three sensors that were attached with adhesive to a zinc strip. He then quickly wrapped the remaining sensors back up and this time placed the package on top of the television set on the back side so it could not be seen. He secured it with an adhesive strip. This would keep it safe until he returned from Denali National Park and could retrieve it. He was amazed at how small the Chinese techs had been able to make the sensor. Other fiber optic communication quantum sensors were much bigger and cumbersome. But these, had been made of a special alloy that allowed the mechanics of the sensor to be very tiny and still operable. Though his specialty was hacking, he understood the mechanics and marveled at the engineering of it.

He remembered what the instructions had said, that he could never be apprehended with any of the package contents so they should be kept somewhere close, but not on him or his belongings. No one would ever think to look at someone else's room, especially that of two middle aged tourists.

He left as quickly as he had come without anyone noticing. He felt proud of himself. So far, things had gone as planned.

Chapter 26

Herman introduced himself.

"Thank you for keeping me from falling." Emma said.

"You're very welcome. Would you do me a favor though?" Herman asked. "Would you have dinner with me?"

Looking him over and knowing she wanted to get to know this man better, Emma didn't hesitate. "I'd love to." She said, as she looked over at Kate. "We'd love to."

Herman looked over at Kate, walked to her and held his hand out. "I'm Herman. It's nice to meet you."

"Kate." she said as she shook Herman's hand.

As Kate dropped his hand, the brown eyed man she had met on the train stepped in behind Herman.

"Well, hello again." He said stepping in front of Herman.

"This is my brother Jim." Herman said. "We are enjoying a retirement vacation. What about you ladies?"

Herman put a gentle arm around Emma and directed her toward the restaurant on the hill at the end of town.

"We are on an adventure, running away from life for a while." Emma explained.

Kate liked that Emma was vague. She was wary of the situation and didn't want to give too many details of their trip away.

Jim stepped over to Kate and held out his hand. "I'm Jim. It's nice to meet you, with your whole face." He said with a wide smile. He was attractive. Without his mask she could see that he wore a five o'clock shadow and had a rugged smile.

"I'm Kate." She said, "It's nice to meet your face too."

Jim continued to smile.

The four walked to the small restaurant near the bottom of the hotel's hill, which was more like a food truck then a café. There were picnic tables outside so they found a table with Kate and Emma sitting on one side and the brothers, Herman and Jim, on the other.

The conversation came easy for Emma. She was thrilled to meet the men and enjoyed their flirtatious banter. Kate hesitated at first, but after some time she let her guard down enough to enjoy the conversation. Herman and Jim were from Anchorage and were on a fishing trip to Fairbanks. Instead of flying or driving, they had decided to take the train south so that they could enjoy a few more days of relaxation before going home.

"We are going into the park tomorrow." Jim said. "Would you like to join us?"

"We are going into the park tomorrow as well." Kate said. Emma explained that they were taking the whole day Denali tour to the mountain.

"Us too. It's settled then. We'll have a fun day together!" Herman said.

Chapter 27

A slight rain began to fall and Herman and Jim offered to walk the two women up the steep hill to their room, but Kate thought better of it.

"That's sweet, but we're good. We'll see you tomorrow on the bus."

"Save me a seat." Jim said with a smile.

The two women pulled up their rain caps and hiked the path to their room near the top of the bluff.

Once back in their room, Kate and Emma started planning for the trip into Denali. Emma washed their masks and a few clothing items in the sink and hung them up to dry in the shower. Kate pulled out the electronic bug repellent watches she had purchased for the trip and plugged them into the charger.

"Well…what do you think of Jim?" Emma asked Kate.

"I don't know. What am I supposed to think of him?"

"Surely, you've noticed that he's swooned by you." Emma teased.

"I'm a fifty something, chubby, graying haired woman. Men don't swoon over me." Kate protested.

"Well, he's swooning over you." Emma responded. "I think you should keep your heart open for another chapter."

"I'll try." Kate said. "You're sure not missing a beat with Herman."

"My heart is open and I'm going to have an adventure!" Emma exclaimed.

"Lucky Herman." Kate teased.

"Well, yes. And lucky me too." Emma chortled.

Chapter 28

As the Alaskan white night turned from shaded to bright again, Kate and Emma rose early and went to breakfast at the restaurant at the hotel. It was a quaint little dining area maintaining the same mountainous outdoorsy theme as the rest of the hotel. Instead of handing them a menu, the young waitress greeted them and asked if they wanted oatmeal or yogurt and fruit for breakfast.

"Are those the only choices?" Kate asked.

"Yeah, our shipment hasn't come in from Anchorage yet so that's what we have to offer. We've got apples and yogurt or oatmeal with raisins, but I can't offer fresh milk. It's tough to get it fresh enough to keep very long up here. We have powdered milk for the oatmeal if you'd like."

Both women ordered the oatmeal. "Ronald loved oatmeal." Emma said reminiscing.

"Oatmeal is what made you think of Ronald?" Kate asked in surprise.

"This entire place makes me think of Ronald. He loved the outdoorsy lifestyle. When we were married, we would go hiking all the time. He was always outdoors doing something. We even had a couple of jousts outside, if you know what I mean." Emma said with a smile.

"I'm sure you did." Kate giggled, amused at Emma's candor. "Some men are just meant to stay outside."

Emma laughed. "I know, and I should've kept him there. Too bad I kept letting him back in." Emma laughed referring to her two marriages to Ronald before they finally called it quits for good.

"At least you can laugh about it." Kate said.

"Why shouldn't I? Ronald was great fun and a great disaster all rolled up in one." Emma explained. "He was never boring. Crazy maybe, but never boring."

Kate admired her friend. Emma always embraced things positively. She was able to laugh and find the good in things, even when times were tough. Kate marveled at her resilience. She needed those traits from Emma to rub off on her.

After enjoying their oatmeal and picking up their pre-ordered lunches from the front desk, the two women went outside above the hotel to wait for the bus at the small cliffside parking lot. There they noticed the sign that showed a dinosaur sized mosquito picking up a man like he was eating a bug. Both women laughed at the sign, but pinned their electronic bug repellent watches to their lapels.

"I'd hate to see what that bug would do when he picked up a grizzly bear." Kate laughed.

Several people gathered near the cliffside parking lot as the morning grew later. The bus pulled up exactly at 9am. Kate and Emma did not see either Herman or Jim before masking and boarding the bus.

"Well, I guess they over slept." Emma said. "Oh well, we'll have a wonderful time either way."

Herman and Jim greeted them as they climbed aboard.

"Good morning!" Herman exclaimed.

"Good morning." Both women said simultaneously.

"We wondered if you'd over slept." Emma said.

"Nope. I'm up with the sun, and it never seems to go down this time of year." Jim joked. "Our cousin is the bus driver, so he took us to breakfast and let us get on early. We have first choice of seats."

Emma and Kate both looked at the driver who tipped his hat to them.

"I'm Gary."

"Good morning, Gary." Kate said.

Emma smiled at him and walked down the isle of the bus to the seats that Herman had saved for the four of them.

"People aren't allowed to drive all the way into the park anymore." Herman explained. "The state is trying to keep everything pristine, but there's just too many people. The best views will be on a bus tour."

Herman and Jim were great tour guides. They shared about the history of Denali National Park and Wildlife Preserve. Though they had both done some research and reading prior to their trip, Kate and Emma both learned a lot from the brothers as they narrated the day.

"Denali National Monument and McKinley National Park combined in 1980. It was the first park that specifically preserved the wildlife." Jim shared.

"It's only called Denali now. They took out the McKinley name because the natives up here had already named it when Washington DC decided to get involved. It just made sense to go back to its original name so the State of Alaska had it all changed." Herman explained.

As Herman was sharing, there was a commotion on the right side of the bus. The bus slowed and as the four turned to look, a large male moose walked along the back of the bus. Its antlers were towering over the windows and Kate was sure that the antlers would at least crack the glass. However, the moose walked gracefully and seemed to dance before gliding back down into the trees by the side of the gravel road.

Kate quickly snapped a couple of pictures with her cell phone.

The bus continued on and soon it breached the taller trees and moved into open space with winding glacial river beds and an open tundra landscape. There were a few sparse trees toward the hilltops, but they were dwarfed and were not much taller than Kate. Suddenly, Emma noticed a large brown figure to the north of the bus.

"What's that?" she asked as she pointed.

Gary stopped the bus and got on the microphone. Speaking quietly, he said, "There is a grizzly to the north of the bus. Please keep quiet so we don't disturb the bear. This time of year, they are feeding and this is a regular feeding spot for them. You can ask questions, but please keep your voices down."

"What do they eat?" someone near the front of the bus asked in a whisper.

"I think he's ripping out a tree stump to look for insects or small rodents. However, they will eat about anything. They are like people. They eat both plants and animals." Gary explained.

The tourists continued to whisper. Sometimes to each other and sometimes asking Gary questions. All were considerate and kept their voices down. The grizzly tore an entire stump from the ground and appeared to be eating small items from it. After it had eaten everything or got his fill, the bear wandered toward the bus.

Gary put his finger over his mouth as if to ask for silence. The tourists complied, all the while spying on the bear and taking pictures.

The grizzly continued its path toward the stopped bus. It sniffed the air several times as if trying to get a location on something. After moving within about ten feet of the north side of the bus, it sniffed something on the ground and then turned and slowly wandered back out onto the tundra covered meadow. Soon it was far from the bus and out of sight.

Kate and Emma both sighed in relief.

"That was exciting!" Kate said, thoroughly enjoying herself.

"It probably smelled how good Emma smells." Herman flirted.

"I am awfully good." She cooed.

Kate rolled her eyes and then laughed out loud. Emma laughed too.

As the bus drew deeper into the park the valley widened even more along with the river bed, with glacial silt and debris. The road became tougher to navigate and at one point had slid completely away into the river below.

"Are we driving over that?" Kate asked.

"It looks like it." Jim answered and looked nervously forward at his cousin behind the wheel.

The bus took a sharp turn into the hillside and traveled down a new makeshift pile of dirt that had been moved to fill in the gaping hole created by the slide. Some of the passengers gasped as Gary carefully dropped the bus about four feet off of the embankment and onto the pile of dirt. He then slammed the accelerator, preventing the bus from getting bogged down in the freshly piled dirt and it lurched forward back on to the gravel on the other side of the slide area.

"Whew!" Jim exhaled. "Way to go, Gary!"

The passengers simultaneously broke out in applause. Gary tipped his head in thanks in the rear-view mirror so that the passengers could see him. He then took the bus to the bottom of the hill and back up the next hill where there was a gravel turnoff large enough to get the bus off of the road.

"We will take a break here." Gary informed them. "Jim and Herman, can you come up here and help me?"

Jim and Herman moved to the front of the bus and deboarded with Gary, while the other passengers, including Kate and Emma, gathered cameras, cell phones, and binoculars before climbing off of the bus.

The spot gave them excellent views of the entire valley, including Mt. Foraker and the distant summit of Mt. Denali. The clouds had haunted them all morning, but it seemed that just as the group stepped out of the bus to look, the clouds cleared and the wide-open view was presented to every onlooker.

"Wow!" Kate said, snapping some pictures of the unbelievable view. "Thank you, God! That was perfect timing."

"You know, Denali is only visible about thirty days a year." Herman said as he and Jim made their way to Kate and Emma.

"Then this is truly a rare day." Kate said.

"Yes, it is." Jim said as he looked directly into Kate's eyes and smiled. "It truly is a rare day."

Blushing, Kate turned away and smiled to herself. Maybe she wasn't "dead" after all.

Chapter 29

Soon, Gary called everyone back to the bus. He asked the group to remain outside of the bus so that he could talk with everyone at once. When all of the passengers had gathered, Gary began. "This is the Polychrome Overlook. You can see that we have a beautiful view of a glacial valley and of the mountains. The largest mountain in the foreground is Mt. Foraker. Denali is the little peak in the back. We'll get a better view of her later in the tour. In the meantime, I have some good news and some bad news."

He continued, "The road that we just traveled over is in pretty bad shape and it won't handle the weight of the bus again the way it is. So, we will go further into the park and extend our tour until later in the evening. By then the road crew will be here and have some time to fill in more gravel so it will withstand the weight of the bus."

He continued. "The good news is, we will get to extend the tour and we won't have to share the road because no other buses are getting through today. The bad news is, that if you had plans tonight, they may have just been cancelled."

"Are you sure we can get back?" one passenger asked.

"Yes, I've driven down the hill in worse shape, but taking the bus down the hill is easier than getting it back up, so we'll have to wait until they can pour some more gravel in there. I've radioed the park road crew and they are on their way."

"What time do you think we'll get back?" another passenger asked.

"I'm not sure, but I promise you will love every minute that you're here." Gary said with a smile before asking everyone to mask up and get back on the bus.

Once aboard and seated, Emma asked, "Did you guys know that the road was out?"

"Gary told us. He was wondering what we should do. He debated about whether to just stay here or continue on. We haven't gotten to the ranger station yet, so we suggested that he just finish the tour rather than wait around for a gravel truck. If we have to stay the night, we'll be better off at the ranger station anyway."

"Stay the night?" Kate asked.

"I doubt it, but if the road crew doesn't get here on time, we may have to."

"Now we can tell our kids we really are roughing it!" Emma retorted. Kate laughed too, but nervously.

"We've been in tougher scrapes then this before Kate. And, at least now we have excellent company." Emma encouraged and looked at Herman.

Kate's anxiety lowered a bit as she thought about the days following the big earthquake in Japan. That certainly was a tough situation and, yes, they had come away from that spring wiser, kinder, and more humble. Emma was right. It would be fine. After all, this was an adventure.

With her lift in spirits, Kate shared about the earthquake with Herman and Jim. She talked about how her husband had converted their gas barbecue to wood so that they could cook. She talked about the evacuations of the thousands of Americans from the Misawa Air Base and how it was all-hands-on-deck getting everyone out and away from the radiation contamination.

The men listened intently as the bus creeped along the gravel road toward the ranger station. When Kate was finished with her story Jim glanced at her wedding ring and asked, "So, Matthew is your husband?"

"Yes…was." Kate dropped her head. "He passed away of cancer."

"Well, that explains the ring." He said, taking a gentle hold of her left hand and looking at it. "I'm so sorry for your loss."

"I haven't had the heart to take my ring off." Kate said.

"If you don't want to, you shouldn't." Jim comforted. "He was important to you. No one else can tell you when you should take your ring off."

"Thank you." Kate said stunned. She appreciated his thoughtfulness.

Chapter 30

The glacial river valley joined two main waterways. The river was full of silt and a light gray color. There were boulders for yards on the river banks and the streams of water diverted into many paths as it wound down the valley. The road, or what you could call a road, was nestled up against a steep cliff. Rocks had fallen onto the gravel and Gary slowed down to drive around most of them. He tried to hang to the outside of the road, trying to avoid any more rockfall if it happened.

"This is the 'safe' option?" Emma joked.

The Toklat Ranger Station was very small compared to those in the Pacific Northwest where Kate and Emma were from. It consisted of one room that was set up to display pictures and artifacts of the area. It was a quaint little museum of sorts with a photo of the first dog sledders in the area, examples of the rock found there, the history of the park, and more. The most interesting to the two women were the antlers that were out for display outside of the building. There was a ranger there telling tourists as they walked by about the different examples of antlers and letting people hold them.

Emma and Kate couldn't help but get in on the action. Emma immediately grabbed the moose rack and, with some effort, hoisted it up toward her head. Kate quickly took a picture and laughed.

"Wow!" Emma said breathing hard as she lowered the rack. "Those are heavy."

Kate grabbed the elk antlers and did the same as Emma had done with the moose rack.

"Now it's my turn." She giggled.

Emma took a shot of her with her cell phone.

"Why don't you both do that together?" Herman said.

Emma quickly handed her phone to Herman and joined Kate. The two women were laughing as they hoisted antlers over their heads in unison as Herman snapped a picture.

After more laughter, Herman walked with the women up the bank of the Nenana River where they admired the rocks and spotted some Dall sheep on the ledge above the opposite side of the river. They continually took pictures.

"I never want to forget this place." Kate said. "It's so lovely here." She picked up her pace and strolled several yards in front of Emma and Herman. She desired a little alone time to think of Matthew.

Chapter 31

The map he was given showed an unmanned communications station on the ridge above Toklat Ranger Station. This station relayed satellite and ground communications between the lower states, the satellites, and the top-secret bases in Alaska, including Clear Station, the ballistic and nuclear missile deterrent station. Otherwise known as the "Spy Base," Clear contained most of the Pentagon's wargame secrets so any communications coming from there could be good information for his contacts in the Communist Party of China. He knew implanting the sensor into the communication station would be risky. He wasn't sure he would have enough time to get there and return to the bus before its departure, which would mean that he would not be able to retrieve the other two sensors and carry out the rest of the mission. The unfortunate damage to the road was good news for him. It meant that the tour could stay longer at the ranger station while they were waiting for repairs to the road.

Chapter 32

Grabbing his red flannel hiking shirt, Jim exited the bus at the ranger station. As he glanced at Gary, he moved his head slightly to indicate that Jim should look in the direction of his nod. Jim, understood, and gazing in the direction Gary nodded, he saw the man heading for the river bank. He watched only briefly before realizing that the man was taking the hiking trail to the ridge. Jim signaled Herman and then jogged quickly up the river bed so that the man wouldn't know he was following. He then traversed the weaving streams of water and began climbing the cliff. He'd not brought any climbing gear with him, but this was the only way that he knew of to get to the top of the ridge without being detected.

At one point, Jim slipped and both feet and one hand came from their grip on the cliff face. He used his body's falling momentum to swing and was able to grab a small hold on the rock face firmly with his loose hand.

"Whew!" he said aloud.

Jim regained his balance and found places for both feet to be firmly on the rock. He was shaking and knew that he needed a couple of seconds to just calm himself. Jim had not climbed competitively for several years and his muscles were screaming at him. About three yards above, he found a platform of sorts where he could stand and catch his breath. Jim was 63 years old and this kind of physical strain was not what he was used to anymore. He thought taking the Anchorage position two years ago would give him a quiet life where he could relax and work at a desk job until he retired. Today, that was not proving to be true.

As he caught his breath, he looked up. There, across the river was a woman staring at him. She waved even. It was then that he realized it was Kate.

"No!" he exclaimed in a whisper worried that someone above him would hear him. He knew he was close to the top of the cliff face so he turned away from the river and quickly bouldered the rest of the way, slowing only when he could see the trail. He ducked among the boulders while he took in the landscape.

It was beautiful here. It was wide open on top, with the Alaskan tundra as far as you could see except the littering of boulders near the cliff. However, there was a manmade metal building near the top of the ridge. He'd been up here a couple of times, but had never seen the new building before. Just then he spotted the man with the Mariners hat about a quarter of a mile down the trail. Jim made sure that he was hidden among the boulders and waited.

Chapter 33

"Matthew would have loved it here." Kate thought. As she walked, she felt as if he was telling her that it was time to move forward. Time to be who she used to be before he got sick. It was time for her to shed her anxiety and trauma from always trying to keep up on his care and be adventuresome again without all of the doubts flooding in. She felt like he was telling her that it was okay to live again.

After being deep in thought for a while, she realized, after looking back down the river, that she had wandered a good distance up the winding waterway, away from the ranger station and from other people. While she wasn't scared, she thought it wise to turn around.

As she turned, she spotted someone on the cliff on the opposite side of the river. It appeared to be a man in a red shirt. He didn't seem to have a rope or climbing protection as he zigzagged up and around boulders on the large escarpment. Kate stood and watched him for a few minutes.

Once, his hand slipped and Kate let out a gasp as she expected him to fall. The man held on and gracefully swung himself back up and gripped the rock again. He soon came to a shelf of sorts and began to look around. He looked straight at her. Though she couldn't make out who the climber was, she waved, thinking the man was proud of his accomplishment and was glad to have had a witness to it. However, the man seemed startled and quickly ran up over the remaining rock and out of sight.

"That was weird." She said to herself aloud, making a mental note to share her observations with Emma.

Chapter 34

He looked down the trail to make sure that he hadn't been followed, but second guessed himself. He could see the metal communication station. It was right where he'd been told it was. It looked out of place and he wanted to be away from it as soon as possible. He released the fanny pack he was wearing and pulled out a screw driver. Using the tool, he took off the lower left panel on the north side of the structure as his instructions had said. He pulled out the electronic wire grid that he had exposed and took the sensor and placed it in the cavity. He then put the wire grid back in place, being careful not to dislodge the sensor. He hastily screwed the outside panel back in place and headed back down the hill at a jogger's pace.

Jim watched. He was only about 50 feet from the metal structure. He could tell the man was placing something inside of the building's electronics. What it was, he didn't know.

After the suspect was far enough down the trail to not be seen, Jim rushed to the metal communication station. He desperately wanted to see what the suspect had inserted into the panel. He searched his pockets. He had a few coins and a small pocket knife.

"Bingo." Jim breathed.

Jim used the blade of the small knife to remove several screws from the panel that the suspect had just put in place. Under the panel was an electronic wire grid that partially came out when the panel gave way. Jim was going to push it back in when he noticed that it was not attached in the back. He removed the grid and looked behind it. There was nothing except, stuck with adhesive, was a small metal like patch about the size of a quarter. It looked out of place. Using the tip of the knife blade, Jim pried the round object off of the metal at the back of the panel.

"What in the world is this?" he said to himself, looking at the small piece of electronics.

Putting the metal like orb in his pocket, he quickly pushed the wire grid back into the building and replaced the panel. Jim did not want the man to see him on the trail but he did not think that he would be able to climb back down the cliff safely. So instead, he traversed the ridge in the opposite direction and joined the trail that went into the valley from the east. This would look as if he was coming from the road instead of the river. This route was longer, however, so he would have to do it at a rapid pace.

Chapter 35

The group spent a couple of hours in the river valley adjacent to the ranger station before Gary asked them all to get back on the bus.

Emma and Kate were one of the first to board. As Kate looked out the window, she saw Herman and Jim coming toward the bus. Jim was wearing a long-sleeved red flannel shirt. Kate noticed it right away because it seemed just like the red shirt she had seen on the climber. Kate continued to watch Jim shed the shirt and quickly stuff it in his daypack before boarding the bus.

Kate didn't say anything to Emma. She was confused and wondered why Jim had gone climbing. She realized that she hadn't seen him since they had arrived at the ranger station, but why had he run when Kate tried to wave hello.

"Did you enjoy your climb?" Kate asked as Jim neared her.

Jim looked stunned and hesitated. "Pardon?" he asked.

"I saw you on the cliff. That's pretty gutsy not wearing a harness or using a rope for protection."

"You saw a climber?" Herman asked. He looked at Jim.

"Yes, and I'm pretty sure it was you." She said pointing at Jim.

"It wasn't me." Jim responded. I was helping Gary with some maintenance stuff on the bus.

"Oh." Kate said apologetically. "I hadn't seen you at the ranger station so I was sure it was you."

"No worries." Jim smiled as he changed the subject. "Did you ladies get to see the Dall sheep?"

Herman and Emma told Jim all about their experience hiking up the river, but Kate was quiet. She was confused. Why did the climber appear to run away from her? She was still fairly certain it was Jim, but why would he lie about something like that? Clearly there were things that she didn't know about. She was mad at herself for not noticing her surroundings better and vowed to pay more attention.

Chapter 36

The tour bus headed deeper into the park. It plodded along through the river valley and down in elevation where the trees were more plentiful and the mosquitos were almost large enough to drag off a man. They pulled over at a primitive picnic area where there were outhouses. The picnic area was forested much thicker than in the higher elevations and had a small calm stream flowing along side. Gary let everyone know that it was a long way to the next bathroom, so he advised everyone to use the outhouses. Emma and Kate took his advice. They were glad for the bug watches. They had worked very well and neither woman had been bitten all day.

The trees and foliage at the picnic area were much different than the tundra. Kate and Emma spent some time trying to identify some of the flowers and plants near the stream while they waited for the other passengers to use the bathroom and stretch their legs. They walked down a short path leading to a wooden platform where the vista was higher than the running water. Observers could look directly into the stream from above it, giving a bird's eye view of the fish swimming in the smooth clear water. Kate and Emma both enjoyed watching the large trout swim up the stream. At one point, one trout jumped out of the water for an insect.

"If he caught a mosquito, he got a big meal." Kate giggled.

Both women chuckled.

Chapter 37

The bus traveled through more beautiful tundra along the river until it came to a pass. At the top, there was a large pullout. Over the speaker, Gary announced, "This is the Stony Hill Scenic Overlook. If the weather is our friend today, you should be able to see a very close view of Denali."

Kate and Emma, along with most of the passengers, got off of the bus to view the landscape. The day was cloudy, but again, right as they were about to give up hope of seeing the summit, the clouds broke away and Mt. Denali could be seen in all her splendor.

"Wow!" Kate said breathlessly.

"Exactly!" Emma chimed in.

They took many pictures, including some selfies for their own keepsakes. At one point a couple asked Kate to take their picture, which she did. So, Kate asked them if they would take a picture of her and Emma. The woman obliged and took Kate and Emma's picture. Since the edges of the pullout were fairly steep the passengers all stayed on the pullout area, which made the space a little crowded. Kate tried to take the couple's picture without other people in it, but with the size of the mountain, it was difficult to snap the photo at exactly the right moment. She was sure that would be the problem for the woman taking their picture as well.

"Don't worry about the other people. If there are others in the shot it's fine with us." She assured the willing photographer.

That's when Kate noticed the man with the Mariners hat. He seemed to be staring at them. She tried to brush the bad feeling away, but it nagged at her. She reminded herself that she needed to pay close attention to him from now on.

Chapter 38

The day was long. Gary, the driver, determined not to have to stay the night in the park, drove the passengers back to the part of the road that had been damaged. There was a crew working on the road. They had dumped more gravel on the caved-in section, but Kate and Emma weren't so sure it would still hold the bus.

Gary seemed to agree. He stopped the bus on the hillside and got out to talk to one of the road crew members. He then came back to the bus and asked all of the passengers to walk across the damaged area because he thought that would be safer than riding in the bus.

Gary, with the help of the road crew, then attached two large chains to the front of the bus and attached them to a heavy tractor brought by the road crew. The passengers gathered their things and walked up the hill. The road was clearly stable enough for human traffic, but no one seemed sure if it was safe for a heavy bus.

Gary got behind the wheel and slowly drove upward with the chain torqued tight against the moving tractor. As the bus moved onto the soft part of the new roadway it sank slightly, but not enough to get stuck. Gary did not stop. He continued the bus in the upward motion until its rear tires had cleared the damaged area by 100 feet or so.

After parking the bus, he got out and told the awaiting passengers to again load the bus for the final miles back to Denali Townsite. Kate and Emma were relieved.

"Well, that was exciting!" Herman mused as he boarded. "Didn't you think so Emma?"

"Yes, I guess so, but I think I'm done with the excitement for today." The ride into Denali Townsite was quiet. Most of the passengers were sleeping, as the day had gone long and it was getting late. The sun had dipped below the skyline and back up again, before they arrived at the hotel.

Chapter 39

The women were tired and decided to skip breakfast so they could sleep a few minutes longer before going back to the train. They took their time gathering their things before leaving their room. Both women took their keycards with the intension of taking them back to the check-in desk before they left. However, Emma realized, once they'd gotten to the lobby, that she had left her cell phone on the night stand. The clerk told her to just leave her keycard in the room on the TV stand and housekeeping would recover it there.

"I'll be right back." She said to Kate as she left for the room. Kate remained in the lobby with all of their belongings.

***

He was growing impatient waiting for the women to leave their room. It would leave precious little time for him to come up with a plan to hide the package again. He had been lingering in the picnic area near their room door for a half hour and it was starting to look suspicious, before he saw the two women finally exit their room.

As soon as they were up the stairs toward the lobby he quickly used his key coder and slid inside the room. Going over to the TV, he was relieved that the small package he had placed earlier was still there.

He spotted a cell phone on the night stand between the two beds.

"This will work." He improvised. He removed the cell phone case, opened the small package and stuck the two small discs in the cell phone case lining, and snapped the cover back on the phone. He would turn it into the desk at the lobby and say he found it on the ground.

Just as he clicked the cover back on to the cell phone, the door clicked indicating that the lock had been opened. He dove for the wall and rolled himself up against the bed that was furthest from the door.

"I'll be right there!" He heard her holler to someone in the distance.

He could see her feet as she came into the room, leaving the door open.

"Now, where is it?" She said aloud.

He realized that she was looking for the phone. He was still holding it. He silently slid it under the bed to the other side, hoping she would spot it on the floor, pick it up, and leave.

***

Emma was trying to hurry but she had to find her cell phone. She was sure she had left it on the night stand between the beds in their room. She didn't see the phone immediately so she began to scan the room trying to think where she last had it. She instantly thought that she may have knocked it off of the stand in her haste to leave so she looked on the floor.

She spotted the phone just under the edge of her bed.

"There it is." She said aloud.

She bent down to pick it up when she noticed that the case to her phone was not on solidly. She snapped the corner tight and ran out of the room closing the door behind her. She continued to run until she reached the lobby.

***

He could see her shoes moving quickly across the wood floor and the door going shut again.

Hesitantly, he looked out around the end of the bed. He went to the door and slowly opened it and looked around before exiting.

"Oh, my God!" he thought. "That was close."

He didn't know what he would have done if the woman would have spotted him. His heart was pounding.

Chapter 40

Kate and Emma were glad to board the train again. They enjoyed living in the lap of luxury. The meals were made restaurant style, each car had its own tour guide/steward, the seats were wide and had plenty of room to stretch out, and best of all, there was a 180° view. Yesterday had been a long day and they were looking forward to a leisurely ride to Anchorage.

In only ten short miles, the train twisted and turned its way through forests to the Continental Divide where at 2,363 feet, they had a spectacular view of Summit Lake which eventually drained into both the Pacific Ocean and the Bering Sea. Both were surprised that they were at such a low elevation, since all other Continental Divide passes in the west were higher.

On the south side of the pass, the forests cleared and they had wide open views of the surrounding mountains. It seemed like the mountains went on forever. Most were snow covered and rugged. It reminded both of them of northern Japan and the Hokado Mountains. There were steep canyons and sheer cliffs. And then the contrast of harsh landscapes with the peacefulness of the wilderness. It was breathtaking!

Both women were keeping their phones close because everything was so beautiful and they were taking pictures frequently.

After they had traveled about forty-five miles, the train began to move down a mountainside. As it moved around a blind corner a bridge suddenly appeared. It seemed like the bridge went on past their viewpoint. Their guide told them that it was actually 918 feet and crossed the steep canyons of a creek that was almost 300 feet below. The train slowed so that everyone could get a long view as they crossed the bridge. To their left, on the inside of the canyon, the creek exploded from the mountainside as a raging waterfall before landing in a small pool far below that was barely visible from the bridge. To their right, the creek fell down the canyon which opened up into a vast meadow with high peaks beyond. Both women were amazed.

"Is every place in Alaska breathtaking?" Kate asked her friend.

"Wow." Was all Emma could say.

Chapter 41

The train arrived in Talkeetna before noon. Some passengers disembarked as their travels ended for the day. As well, some passengers boarded as they had stayed in Talkeetna and were going on to Anchorage.

Jim and Herman did not want to raise suspicion with the man they were surveilling. They didn't think that he realized that he was being followed and they didn't want to tip him off. As planned, agent and former Army Coronel, Margie Youngblood, would be keeping an eye on the suspect on the train between Talkeetna and Anchorage. Jim pretended that he did not notice Agent Youngblood board the train. Instead, he and Herman took a few minutes to say goodbye to Kate and Emma.

"It was very enjoyable in the park yesterday. Thank you for joining us, even though it lasted longer than you'd expected." Herman said reaching his hand out to Emma.

"It was enjoyable." Emma responded.

Jim reached for Kate's hand as well and she shook it and thanked him for being a great tour guide in the park.

Jim turned to go, but Herman hesitated. "May I have your phone number, Emma? I would love to keep in touch."

Emma blushed. "Of course. I'd like that too."

The two exchanged phone numbers before Herman followed Jim off of the train.

***

A couple of miles beyond Talkeetna, as Kate was facing downward looking at the pictures she had just taken on her phone, Emma elbowed her.

"Look."

As the train came to a stop, in front of them, was a monstrous group of high glacial mountains. Standing so tall they looked like they reached outer space; Mount Denali, Mount Foraker, Mount Russell, and Mount Dall stood before them like a vast curtain in the skyline. Again, both women took pictures with their phones.

"Stunning." Emma said.

"I could look at this view forever." Kate said.

Both women were struck by the vastness of it all. The graying blue mountains rose into pillars of white as they jutted upward toward the heavens. Then there were waves of dark white glaciers rolling from the peaks to the lowest valleys. Waterfalls boiled further down the draw, carved by prehistoric glacier flows, turning to ripples where three rivers joined together. They were disappointed when the train began to move.

As they grew closer to Wasilla the landscape had fewer trees and appeared to be marshy like wetlands. Wasilla seemed like a quiet frontier town.

"I can see Russia from my house." Kate mused as she imitated Tina Fey's *Saturday Night Live* impression of Sarah Palin, who was a former vice-presidential candidate from Wasilla. Both women laughed.

Chapter 42

Past Wasilla the scenery opened up to the Matanuska area, which was flatter and they could actually see a few farm fields. It seemed like they were in a coastal region now. While there were mountains to the north and east, southward looked like an open plain.

Soon they arrived at Elmendorf Air Force Base where the train slowly glided by the airfield. The women loved the air planes. A fighter jet took off. Kate always loved the sound of the fighter jets. It brought back memories of her time in Misawa. At the building where she worked, they were close enough to the runway to hear when the fighter jets went airborne. The loud roaring of the jet engines seemed powerful. It helped that she knew most of the fighter pilots in Misawa. She so admired their skills and talent.

When Kate mentioned this to Emma the two reminisced about the time when Emma flew in a hornet with the Navy off the coast of Japan. Kate had been in the crow's nest of the aircraft carrier with the Pacific Admiral at the time and watched her land in the passenger seat, with a top gun Navy pilot at the helm.

"What a thrill that was." Emma shared.

"Good memories." Kate stated.

Before they knew it, they could see the Cook Inlet. The train slowed and creeped into the Anchorage Train Station, which was close to the water. After departing the train, Kate and Emma could see the bay, the marina, and some of the downtown area of Anchorage. Kate looked up the address for their bed and breakfast while Emma busily took pictures.

"Let's cue up for a taxi." Kate told her friend.

Both snapped their smaller daypacks onto the outside of their backpacks and hoisted everything onto their shoulders. Neither woman noticed the man in the Mariners hat watching them.

***

The taxi meandered a few blocks uphill from the train station, through a couple of alleyways and into a carport. There was a small quaint sign that read, "Artic Fox."

"We are here." The taxi driver announced.

"That wasn't very far from the station." Kate noticed.

"No, we only came a half of a mile."

Both women giggled at themselves, knowing that they could have walked rather than spend the taxi fare.

The driver helped them get their backpacks from the trunk before leaving. Kate walked up the flight of stairs to the door and rang the bell.

The owner, Kevin, was a tall man with a broad smile. "Kate and Emma, I'm assuming."

"Yes." Kate responded while Kevin opened the door and let them in.

"It's great to meet you face to face. I think you'll love the Artic Fox as much as we do." He said.

The three entered into a large open room on the second floor.

"There's everything you need to cook on this side." Kevin said as he waved his arm toward the kitchen area. "There are some snacks provided on the counter." As he led them further into the main room, he pointed out the seating area and the bathrooms that were open to everyone. He motioned toward the doors to the sleeping rooms, and then led them to the front of the house. The door they entered opened to an adorable double room. The two windows were large and let in a bright amount of sunlight.

"I'd say you have the afternoon sun in here, but everybody has the sun in Alaska this time of year." Kevin joked.

All of them laughed.

"Please settle in. If you have any questions, please let me know. My partner and I live downstairs and are available whenever you need us."

"Thanks so much." Kate said. "Is there a restaurant close so that we can get some dinner?"

"Oh yes, there are many." Kevin replied. "Downtown is only about 4 blocks and there are many restaurants there. My favorite is going topside at the 49th State Brewing. They have great food and a great view."

***

The women didn't go to a popular hotel. Where were they going? He had cued for a taxi right after the two women and had the driver follow them at a distance. When they pulled in, the other taxi was pulling out of the Artic Fox driveway. He told the driver to turn around and take him back down the hill toward the train station. The driver seemed confused, but complied.

Once out of the taxi, he walked back up the hill staying close to the buildings so he wouldn't be spotted. Surveying the property of the bed and breakfast, he slowly circled it, watching to make sure no one knew he was there. When he was done, he was discouraged. The only door to the upper bed and breakfast, which opened into a main room, was a key lock, which meant it would take a few minutes for him to manually pick the lock to access the door. His electronic key coder would not work. In addition, the owner of the property was there in the large main room on the lower floor watching television. He would easily be spotted if he went to the upper door.

His only choice, for now, was to wait until the women left. He found some hedges along the street and waited.

Chapter 43

Kate and Emma were eager to get out and explore Anchorage. Neither had been there before and Kate particularly wanted to see the fish run at Ship Creek. She had seen fish run before. As a child, growing up near the wilderness area of northern Idaho, she often saw the salmon coming from the ocean up area creeks to spawn. However, as the salmon population had severely declined during her lifetime, the fish couldn't be seen much anymore. And, if you could see them, there were so few it wasn't clear if the fish were traveling to spawn or simply just there. Kate remembered one early November, when she was eighteen years old, coming across a creek that was so loaded with red Sockeye that she could not walk across the stream without stepping on one. It had amazed her so much at the time that she had wanted to see that again.

Looking at the area map, the two decided to walk up toward town to find dinner rather than down by the water to the 49th State Brewery.

"Perhaps we will eat at the brewery tomorrow after we've had our fun." Emma said.

They left the Artic Fox and walked up Third Street and then took a left on "C" Street. There they spotted a sign that said, "Sullivan's Steakhouse."

As they walked across the pavement, Kate looked back to make sure she would be familiar with the route back to the Artic Fox after dinner. That's when she spotted the man with the Mariners hat.

"That's weird." She said to Emma. "Isn't that the same guy that we were on the train with?"

Emma turned around and stopped. "Yes, I believe that it is. Is he staying at the Artic Fox too?"

The man stopped as they turned toward him.

Chapter 44

He would keep his distance, but not let the two women out of his sight. He wasn't sure how he was going to get the cell phone, but he would figure that out once he was closer to them.

As the two women crossed the road to go up "C" Street they stopped and turned around to look at him. He stopped. Without wanting to look suspicious, he gave a slight wave and continued walking toward them. They were waiting for him.

"Great." He thought to himself. "What do I say?"

Thinking quickly as he walked, he said hello when he was in earshot.

"Hello." One of them said. "Didn't you just come off of the train from Denali?"

"Yes," he said. "I thought I'd walk around and see a bit of Anchorage this evening."

"Are you staying at the Artic Fox?" the other woman asked.

"Where?" He was thinking fast. "Uhm, no. I'm at the Hilton." He said pointing up the hill toward the hotel sign. "Where are you headed?" he asked casually.

"Trying to find a place to get dinner." One of them replied. "We were thinking about going to the steakhouse up there."

"Steak sounds like a good choice." He responded. "Enjoy your dinner." He did not want the women to know he was following them so he started to walk again, but continued up Third Street instead of turning up "C" Street where the women were going.

***

Kate and Emma turned and walked up "C" Street the two blocks to Sullivan's Steakhouse. It was a cute little establishment with a small foyer and about ten tables. There was a large wooden carved grizzly bear in front of the window by the door. They were early for an evening meal so the restaurant did not have many patrons in it. The hostess escorted them to a table in the back near a window where they had a clear view of the street.

"This is a cute place." Emma said. "I hope the food is good. I'm starving."

"Anchorage is much smaller than I expected." Kate said. "I think we could walk around the downtown area and see most of it in just a couple of hours. Shall we do that tomorrow?"

"That sounds lovely." Emma responded just as the waitress came to take their dinner order.

As they finished dinner, Kate began to examine the restaurant more closely. It had a frontier rugged charm. She loved the carved grizzly and wanted a picture of it. She held out her camera and aimed it toward the carving in front of the window. As she snapped her first shot, she noticed the man with the Mariners hat sitting at a table near the door.

"He's here now." She said to Emma.

Emma looked up and said, "Is he following us?"

Both women began to get uneasy.

"I'm not sure, but this is our cue to leave." Kate said.

Chapter 45

He knew where they were going now and he'd had time to think of a plan for getting the phone from the smaller woman. He slowed his pace a bit so he would not arrive at the steakhouse too soon.

He arrived as the women were finishing dinner. He asked to be seated at the table nearest to the door. As the women left the restaurant, he said to them, "I took your advice. This looks like a great place to eat. How was it?"

"Really yummy." The smaller woman said, turning to leave.

Noticing that she had her phone in her hand, he stood from his table and asked, "Would you like me to take your picture in front of the grizzly?"

She hesitated briefly. "That would be lovely." She said and handed her phone to him.

"Just go stand in front of it." He instructed.

He turned his back quickly, snapped off the case, and removed one of the sensors that he had hidden in the woman's phone case before he quickly snapped the case back on. When the case snapped on, the phone locked up. He quickly turned back around innocently and held out the phone.

"I must've hit something because it locked up on me."

The smaller woman took the phone, used a number code to unlock it, and handed it back to him. "Here you go." She said.

He quickly snapped a picture of the two of them and handed the phone back to her. "Thanks." She said to him.

"My pleasure." He said.

Chapter 46

As they walked east on Fifth Street Kate and Emma noticed the beautiful bouquets of flowers in front of the log cabin building at the other end of the block. They walked toward it and discovered that it was the Chamber of Commerce building that had brochures about things they could do in Anchorage. Kate began looking through the brochures.

Emma noticed the trolley immediately as it was coming toward the building. When it stopped and the passengers had gotten off, Emma asked the driver when the next tour was.

"This is the last one today, but I start up again tomorrow. There's one every hour until 5:00pm." The woman driver told her.

After thanking her, Emma told Kate about the trolley tours. "I think we should take a tour tomorrow. That will take us to all of the tourist sites in Anchorage and we won't have to pay for a cab or rent a car."

"That is a great idea."

Inside the building, Kate and Emma bought post cards and trinkets for their grandchildren and took a city map and a trolley tour brochure from the "FREE" shelves near the door before heading back to the Artic Fox.

Chapter 47

He got one of the sensors, yet he wondered if he should have taken both of them. He reasoned with himself that the women were easy to follow and he couldn't risk having both of the sensors on him if he were caught. His dinner was served just as the women left the restaurant. He ate the steak so that no one would question why he was there.

After eating he walked up the hill to the Hilton Hotel. He went into the underground parking structure and scanned the area looking for security cameras and older cars that he might be able to easily hotwire. There was a security camera to his far left as he walked into the garage, so he turned right walking far enough that the camera was no longer in sight. He couldn't see any other cameras.

"That's just like Alaskans." He thought to himself. "Everyone up here thinks they are totally safe."

As he spotted an older model Buick, he remembered a conversation that two passengers were having on the flight to Fairbanks. He had overheard them both bragging about the fact that they didn't need a home security system because they carried a gun. He smiled at the thought now, knowing that it wouldn't take a gun to take an old Buick from right under someone's nose.

He picked the lock of the old car quickly and reached under the steering compartment and hotwired the car. He guessed it would be morning before anyone would notice that the car was gone, and he would have it back by then. No one would be the wiser.

He did not notice the woman watching him from the shadows.

Chapter 48

Once back at the Artic Fox, Kate and Emma put on their pajamas and began to relax. The big fluffy chairs in the main room were perfect for reading. After getting some hot tea, Kate pulled out a book she had brought with her and Emma checked her cell phone for messages from her kids.

Emma felt it first. A startled second later she looked to confirm her worst fears. The ceiling fan was moving. It was an earthquake!

Kate looked up as well and said, "It could be that we were on the train all day, but I have sea legs." Noticing that Emma was staring at the ceiling fan and had a look of shock on her face, she looked at the ceiling fan.

"It's not sea legs!" Kate exclaimed. She immediately looked at her watch so she could time the tremor.

The shaking did not stop quickly and grew in intensity. Neither woman got under furniture or moved toward the door. They had learned in Japan that the best thing to do, if you aren't close to a door, is to ride it out. The Japanese even believed that you should get on the floor or ground and be silent.

"The earth should talk, not you." Kate remembered her Japanese friend telling her.

The pictures on the walls began swaying and they could hear the dishes in the kitchen area clattering. Emma was terrified and could not speak.

"Emma, Emma, it's alright." Kate kept reassuring her friend.

After three and a half minutes the shaking began to slow and calm.

"We are alright." Kate said.

Emma shook her head, "yes" and took a deep breath. "How big was that? Will there be a wave?"

"I don't know how big, but it lasted a LONG time. We have to assume that a wave is coming somewhere." Both women began looking on their phone on the National Geological Society's (USGS) website to see if the Richter size had been recorded there yet.

As they were doing that, the owner, Kevin, came into the main room. "Everybody okay up here?" he asked.

Just then Emma saw that the USGS website had listed the earthquake as an 8.3 on the Richter Scale. "It was a big one!" She exclaimed.

"The epicenter must be a long way off because that wasn't even close to an 8.3 where we are standing." Kate said. "Does it say where the epicenter was?"

"It says just off of Korovin Island. There is a tsunami warning issued." Emma responded.

Kate quickly opened the map that they'd taken from the Chamber of Commerce and looked for Korovin Island. Once she found it, she put her finger on it. "Look Emm," she said, "Korovin Island is hundreds of miles from here."

Kevin piped in. "Yes, I'd guess that's about 5oo miles. It's in the Aleutians. And don't worry," he continued, "The Artic Fox is much higher than people realize. It's about 120 feet above sea level here. Unless the quake is close to us, the wave would never get this high."

"Okay?" Kate looked at her friend.

"I guess so, but you know how much I hate those things." Emma responded.

"Yes, I do. And...you were right. I told you that there wouldn't be any quakes while we were here, but you were right."

Another couple came from their sleeping quarters into the main room. While Emma could not talk during the quake itself, she was finding a great deal of anxiety relief sharing all about it now. She told the couple about the size and distance of the quake. She shared about the tsunami warning and what that could look like based on her experiences in Japan. While she was talking, Kate noticed that the tsunami warning had been lifted, which meant there was no longer a risk of a wave coming. That relieved both women, since they knew that many more deaths came from the wave then from the actual earthquake in Japan.

It took both women a couple of hours to settle enough to want to sleep, but when they did, both slept right through two aftershocks that were above a 6.0 on the Richter Scale.

Chapter 49

He wanted to drive fast, but didn't want to catch the attention of any do-gooder citizen who might call in a speeding car, so he tried to keep it at the speed limit. He took Highway One to Sutton, then drove north to Little Granite Creek. The daylight was fading, but he remembered the well-hidden turn off in the trees in order to get to the fiber optic complex.

He had studied the plans of the complex and knew right where he wanted to plant his device. If the layout was correct, he could hide his car in the grove of trees and walk in about 300 yards by foot to access the coded locked gate.

The complex was located along Granite Creek, quietly nestled up against the steep hillside. The creek was swift there and made a gradual waterfall along the south side of the complex. The sound of the brisk water covered up any small noise that he might make.

As he reached the gate, the ground began to move. He looked around to see if he was standing on something unstable, but quickly realized that an earthquake was occurring. He ducked down behind the gate, hoping that he would not be seen as he waited for the quake to pass. The ground shook harder and above him he could see that a large tree was loosening in the soil and about to give way. He quickly ran out in the open meadow just as the tree released and fell down the embankment where he had just been. After the tree, the hill began to slide. The earth was still shaking so it seemed that more and more earth slid down the mountainside to the complex.

By the time the shaking stopped, the gate that he was hoping to access was blocked by rocks, mud, and the large tree that had fallen. With only about an hour of dusk this time of year, he knew he would not have time to clear the gate and do what needed to be done. He needed another plan. This would have to wait until tomorrow.

Slinking back to the car, hotwiring it, and driving it back to Anchorage took about an hour and a half. The earthquake created an unforeseen problem. He hoped his contacts would understand.

Chapter 50

"Our guys say the device that I retrieved from the communication system above Toklat Ranger Station is a quantum interference fiber optic sensor designed to intercept any communications concerning one of our weapons systems, that evidently, I don't have enough clearance to know about." Jim said sarcastically. "Looks like the sensor was made by the Chinese and very effective at stealing information...highly sensitive information."

Jim knew that Herman would understand the message he was reading. He continued, "The device is capable of stealing and analyzing written, audio, electronic, or computer sensitive information as well as disrupting our own communications."

Jim continued to explain the message concerning the fiber optic project of Alaska. It was designed to offer broadband to remote villages...at least that's how they sold it to the public. Covertly, it was a highly classified military weapons communication system that was capable of synching with any electronic device on earth and any orbiting satellite, under the guise of getting high speed internet to remote communities. It was so secret that even the crew on the ground did not know of the extra fiber optic plans that were to be included in the project.

Most of the project's top secret tech personnel were working out of Clear Air Force Base, but there were a couple of high security personnel working within the complex itself, just outside of Sutton, Alaska, in order to provide on-site quality control and security.

Jim had remembered something in the news about the project which was mostly funded by the federal government on behalf of the Alaskan tribal entities in order to get high speed broadband to remote reservation communities. Now he knew, that was only a ruse to cover up the truth.

"What is this Herm?" Jim asked, referring to the message he was reading.

"Jim, it's time that I fill you in on a few things." Herman responded.

Herman told Jim that the sensor could synch with a new potent weaponized satellite communications system and that it was highly classified. It was imperative that they intercept "Mr. Mariner" before the Chinese do and find out how much information and data has been intercepted already. Herman shared with Jim that when the military intercepted a "tourist" on Wainwright Army Base trying to plant one of these sensors, they realized how advanced the technological espionage capabilities of the Chinese were becoming at infiltrating American weaponry, communications, and data.

"So, our guy is trying to communicate with our war satellites?" Jim asked. "What would make a United States Airman betray his country to do this?"

"Money and revenge." Herman responded.

The complication, at least how Jim saw it, was that if they knew that "Mr. Mariner" had the sensors to hack this specialized system, then certainly the Chinese knew as well.

Jim knew there were strategically placed military bases in Alaska that were used to test new weapon systems. Fort Wainwright possessed a tactical command center with nuclear capable artillery. Fort Greely was home to the Ground-based Midcourse Defense System that could intercept and destroy any missiles in flight that were fired at the United States. Point Barrow was used by the U.S. Navy Submarines for discreet communication, sonar networks, and satellite relays. In addition, the Alaska Range was used extensively to covertly test ballistic missiles, nuclear powered aircraft, and space-launch systems. The Tanana Flats was the location of military weapons testing including electromagnetic pulse weapons and directed-energy weapons, which were highly classified technology. But most importantly, Clear Air Force Base housed the most innovative technology concerning fiber optic communication and quantum converters. The infiltration of the station's communication tower relays to the weapons' satellites could be devastating to the US progression of military power, which could change the balance of power in the region.

"What does HQ want us to do about it, is the question." Herman responded.

"And, how many of these little suckers does our 'Mr. Mariner' have?" Jim continued.

Just then Herman received a text.

"It's from Agent Youngblood. She needs to meet with us." He said, as he grabbed his jacket.

Chapter 51

When they woke in the morning and discovered that they'd slept through the larger aftershocks, both laughed as they remembered the seemingly never-ending aftershocks in Japan that they joked about "rocking them to sleep."

Once up, showered, and dressed Kate and Emma walked back to the Chamber of Commerce and signed up for the first trolley tour. They only had to wait about 15 minutes for the trolley to arrive.

"So glad you could join us this morning." The driver said to the familiar Emma. "You can sit wherever you want."

Emma and Kate took a seat in the middle of the open car. It seemed that people came out of the woodwork to get on the trolley. The car was fully loaded when it pulled away from the curb a few minutes later.

The trolley first took them to Ship Creek where the tour guide and driver, an elementary school teacher from Anchorage, had them all get off of the car and walk to the bridge over the creek. Once on the bridge Kate could see the mass of King salmon beneath her. It took her breath away just like it had done so many years ago.

"Matthew would have loved seeing this." She said to Emma.

Kate stayed on the bridge as long as she could before the driver told them to get back on the trolley.

The next stop on the trolley was the Anchorage Airport where a mother moose had two calves she was caring for in the clearing near the runway. The driver explained that the moose was there most days, but sometimes she would go into the trees where spectators couldn't get a glimpse of her or her rare twins.

From there they rambled around Lake Hood doing a drive-by of numerous float planes, with the driver explaining that most Alaskans have their pilot's license before they have their driver's license and that learning how to fly a plane is part of the technical classes at the area high school.

She then drove them to Earthquake Park, which under the circumstances, was a popular desired destination for most of the passengers. She explained that this was the area that was devastated during the 9.2 earthquake that hit Anchorage in 1964.

As the trolley pulled away from the park, Emma's phone made a "ding" sound. She glanced at it quickly and then excitedly said to Kate, "It's Herman."

"What did he say?"

"It says, 'Only been a couple of days, but I miss you already. I'll be in Anchorage today. Dinner?'"

"Where? Time?" Emma texted back without asking Kate.

"What are you telling him?" Kate inquired.

"I asked him when and where." Emma smiled.

At first, Kate was a little agitated, but then realized that this was one of the reasons why she loved Emma so much. The woman could befriend anyone and Kate wanted to be more like that.

"Okay." Kate said.

Chapter 52

The 49th State Brewery was located in an old brick building on the waterfront. It had been remodeled and was now the trendy place to be in Anchorage. There were relics of Alaska's history throughout the building, including old mining tools, photos, and information displays, much like a museum.

Herman had reserved them all a table on the upper level, which Kate was sure was on the top of the old building. The waiter led her and Emma up the stairs…two floors…through a small door that entered the rooftop. It was decorated with modern décor, furniture, and kerosene gas heaters to keep the guests warm and the mosquitos away. Small patio lights were hung by brass figurines that Kate was sure were made by local artisans.

Not surprisingly, when Emma and Kate arrived at the table Jim was there as well as Herman.

"I didn't think you would mind if I brought some company." Herman said as he motioned his arm to Jim.

"Not at all." Emma said.

Herman stood to greet them and pulled a chair out next to him for Emma.

Jim stood as well and pulled a chair out next to him.

"Would you like to sit here, Kate?"

"Good to see you again, Jim." Kate said as she sat down.

The view was spectacular on the rooftop. There was a full view of the harbor and the train station from their table, as well as a skewed view of the Arctic Fox. Though they had agreed to meet Herman and Jim at 8:00pm the Alaskan white night had allowed a bright clear view without clouds. Kate felt like she could breathe with full and open lungs up here. She loved it.

***

The four had good conversation and a good meal, and before Kate realized it, the time had slipped away. The day was beginning to fade, which meant that it must be nearing 11 o'clock.

"Excuse me just for a minute. I'd like to see if I can get a full view of our bed and breakfast before it gets too late. I'm just going to step over to the other side of the rooftop." Kate said to the others.

"I'll come with you." Jim offered.

The two made their way over to the northwest side of the roof where there was a place for guests to stand and get a clear view of the city.

"Our B and B is over there." Kate said pointing northward. As she did, she noticed Jim looking downward to the street below. There, on the sidewalk, was the man in the Mariners hat. The same man who they had seen yesterday.

"That guy showed up when Emm and I had dinner last night."

"He did?" Jim said with a worried look on his face. "Did he talk to you?"

"Yes," Kate said, and then shared the story about how he had come up behind them before dinner and showed up at the restaurant the previous night, offering to take their picture. "He actually locked up Emma's phone trying to take our picture."

Jim's face and demeanor changed. Without saying another word, he hurried back toward the table.

"We have to go Herman." Jim said when he reached the table. "I'm so sorry ladies, but Herman and I need to go now to tie up some loose ends."

Herman seemed surprised, but responded to Jim when he talked with urgency. He took his napkin from his lap and put it on the table, rising up to meet Jim's eyes. He threw some cash on the table to cover the bill and apologized as he and Jim rushed away.

After following Jim back to the table, Kate stood with a stunned look on her face. When the men were gone, she noticed Emma had the same stunned look. After a moment, Emma asked Kate, "What was that about?"

"I don't know. That guy with the baseball hat that followed us and then showed up when we had dinner last night, is on the sidewalk downstairs. When I noticed him, I shared with Jim what happened yesterday, and he didn't say anything, just rushed over here and swished away."

"Okay, this is weird." Emma said as she took out her phone and sent a text to Herman.

"Huh?" her text read.

"Well, it looks like they've covered dinner. We should head back to the B and B so we can get some rest before our train tomorrow." Emma snuffed. "That was fun while it lasted."

"I agree that something weird is going on here." Kate said as the two began walking back to the Arctic Fox. "I didn't tell you this before, but I saw Jim rock climbing the cliff below the ridge at the ranger station in Denali National Park. The climbing itself didn't seem weird, but when I saw him and waved, he seemed like he didn't want to be seen. He denied climbing, but I know it was him."

"Then I guess it's good that we'll part ways with them." Emma said, growing a little more mad with each step. "I don't know why I like men so much. They get you all excited and then just let you down."

At hearing Emma's words, Kate knew she was angry. Trying to lighten the mood a little she said, "Yeah, but they are sure fun when they're not letting you down."

Emma huffed and then took a deep breath and sighed. "You're right. Let's just continue our adventure."

Chapter 53

Frustrated that the earthquake had thwarted his chance at planting the sensor on the fiber optics system yesterday and preventing him from retrieving a node, he knew he had to try again. There was very little darkness in the night sky now so his opportunity to access the fiber optic complex was in a short time span. He was hoping his luck was changing as he found the same old Buick in the parking lot under the Hilton Hotel. It was easy to get into it and start it. And, as luck would have it, the owner had just filled the gas tank.

His contact would be expecting him at the marina in an hour so he drove down near the marina to a nearby restaurant and parked the car. He left the engine running so that, once he met his contact, he could leave quickly and not risk being seen.

At the marina, his contact was late. He hated standing out in the open, but there was no other way to communicate that he hadn't placed the sensor at the fiber optics complex yet. He noticed the boat, "Argentina," was moored on the third dock and the interior lights were on. Rather then wait for his contact to appear, he walked down the dock and stepped aboard.

He heard, "Stop right there. I have a rifle pointing at your temple."

He could not see anyone, but he could see the tip of what he thought was an AK47 sticking out of a port window and aimed at him.

He stopped immediately. "I'm here to see Wu."

"Who are you?"

The man explained that he was to see Wu to give him something, but that he was unable to obtain the item.

"I should have it by tomorrow though." He continued.

"Stay right there." The voice said.

The tip of the rifle remained in the port hole and he could hear two people quietly talking, but could not make out the words.

Soon the voice returned, "Six in the morning tomorrow. If you don't have it, I won't warn you about the rifle. I'll just shoot."

"Understood." He said and made his way off of the boat and down the dock to the restaurant.

He stood briefly on the sidewalk, contemplating his plan for the night. Once he surmised how he would do what needed to be done, he quickly went to the parking lot and drove the car away up the hill and out of town toward the fiber optics complex.

Chapter 54

Jim ran down the two flights of stairs in the restaurant but slowed when he reached the bottom. He did not want to give the man in the Mariners hat any indication that he was being watched. Herman slowed as well and signaled for Jim to go toward the east side of the lower floor so that they could exit out of the back door.

Once on the street, the Man in the Mariners hat was gone. Knowing that he couldn't have gone far, Herman began walking around the outside of the restaurant casually, pretending that he was looking at the boats in the harbor. Jim caught on and pointed at boats and other things making small talk about them. They noticed the man in the Mariners hat get into an old blue Buick Skylark and drive up the hill toward the Hilton Hotel and take a left on 6th Street.

"He's in the same car as yesterday and headed out of town." Herman said. "I'll bet he's going back to try again."

"Let's go!" Jim replied as the two ran toward their vehicle.

Chapter 55

He drove again above Sutton, trying hard to not draw any attention onto himself. He found the same hidden turn off in the trees to leave the car. Because he didn't know what the facility would be like on this night, he turned the car off but left the wires in place where he needed to connect in order to start the car and make a quick get-away if necessary.

He crept to the complex as the light was fading. Knowing that the gate he had been at last night was probably still in a state of disarray, he chose this time to enter the complex through a side door. This entrance was more risky, as he didn't know who would be inside or where they were located. With the gate, he knew exactly where to turn off the alarms, but he did not know the location of the building alarm through the door he was to go through now.

As he reached the door, it appeared that no one was around. The door was locked as he'd expected, but there was no light for a scanner code.

Was the power out? His luck was improving. While it took longer to pick traditional locks, having no power meant that it was likely that there was no alarm system to disarm. He could get in, get out, and have things done in a matter of minutes.

Once he picked the lock, he slowly opened the door. He heard voices, but could not see anyone. He quietly stepped in and climbed directly above him onto the scaffolding that he knew lined the ceiling of the building. With luck, he could remain on the scaffolding all the way to the control room without being detected.

The inside of the building looked like a warehouse at first glance. The large open room held dozens of large car-sized fiberglass spools along one side. The fiber drawing tower was at the front of the building and he could see that strands of fiber were being produced there, but it was not running now. There were winches of different sizes near the tower and multiple five-gallon cans of chemicals, which he assumed were lubricants and coating for the fibrous cables.

"How do we override anything with no power!" exclaimed one of the workers to another.

"It just figures that Kurt forgot to put gas in the generator. I don't know what he thinks we're going to do up here without it." Another worker said.

He silently slid forward, careful not to make noise or any sudden movements that might draw someone's attention. After what seemed like an hour, but was really just minutes, he reached the top of the control room. There was a door on the ceiling of the room to the scaffolding so he opened the door slowly, checking to see if anyone was in there.

With no power, it was going to be very easy to do what he needed to as long as he wasn't detected. Seeing no one in the control room, he lowered himself quietly to the floor and crept over to a large tube-like part of the wall. He used his screwdriver and opened the control panel with the E437G on it, as he knew that was the one he was looking for. It was located in the far left corner of the tube-like section. Once the panel was open, he took the sensor from his pocket. He quickly attached it to the fiber line and stuck it to the side of the panel. Once he knew that it was secure, he grabbed the red plastic bug-like box that was stuck next to it, but he couldn't remove it from the panel by pulling it. So, he used his screwdriver and, like a crowbar, nudging the small red box until it came loose. He quickly put the red box in his pocket and put the panel back in place.

Now that he had what he needed, he realized that he couldn't reach the ceiling to exit the room. He glanced around the room, and finding a stool, he used it to climb into the ceiling door and back onto the scaffolding. This was not ideal because once someone entered the control room he would be detected. But he had to risk it because walking out through the large room to the main door was out of the question.

He scrambled quietly back across the scaffolding and took a deep breath when he reached the door he had come through without anyone noticing. The three workers in the large room were still bickering about the state of things on the complex. At one point, one of them had gone outside the main door to secure the gate, so he was glad he had chosen the side door.

Once he was clear, he grabbed his pocket to assure that he had the red bug-like box and then sprinted toward his car, hotwired it quickly, and was on the road 32 minutes after he parked.

He was quite proud of himself as he sped down the road. Now to get the last sensor and be done with this.

He saw an empty car parked on the side of the gravel road. "Was that there when I came up?" He asked himself. "I must be careful."

Chapter 56

Jim and Herman followed the man at a distance. They did not want him to be alerted that he had a tail. Twice during the drive to Sutton, they even turned off their headlights so they would not be easily noticed on the road.

Herman shut his engine off and coasted to a turn-out in the road near the grove of trees where the man's car was hidden and then checked his watch. Both men got out of the car and crept to the grove of trees. They watched "Mr. Mariner" as he slipped into the side door of the main building on the fiber optic complex.

After he was in, Jim started to follow.

"No." Herman said. We will wait until he's done. We can't let him know we're here yet. We have to know more about his movements before we intercept him."

Jim shook his head in agreement and quietly backed under the trees again.

Keeping track of the time, Herman and Jim waited for the man to come back out of the building.

"Thirty-two minutes! What was he doing for thirty-two minutes?" thought Herman.

Jim and Herman watched the man run for the hidden car, hot wire it, and take off down the road toward the town of Sutton.

"I'm going to see what he was up to" Herman said, "You keep a tail on him."

"Okay," Jim nodded and ran toward their car.

Chapter 57

Herman went to the main entrance of the complex and flagged down a worker. Identifying himself, he told the worker to call his supervisor and he would explain why he was there.

Once he gained access, Herman went straight to the control room. Immediately, he saw the stool below the open ceiling door. The workers were surprised.

"No one came in here." Said one of them.

"No one you saw." Piped Herman sarcastically.

Herman looked at the tube-like wall with its 12 small panels. The panels were the only easy entrance to the completed cable system. He told the workers that he needed every panel on the tube-like wall opened and to tell him if anything was out of place. None of them argued with him and quickly each got screwdrivers to open the small panel doors on the wall.

"This one!" one worker said who had opened the bottom panel on the left. It looks like they've taped one of the cables and the node is gone.

"Check them all." Herman barked while he picked up the phone on the counter.

***

Jim did not want to spook the man so he followed at a distance, noticing the dust cloud in front of him to determine if the man had turned off of the road. He did not turn on his headlights until he was on the double laned highway on his way back into Anchorage.

As Jim entered cell service, he quickly dialed Agent Youngblood and told her to meet him at the Hilton. He wasn't sure if he needed it, but he wanted some back-up in case things went south in Anchorage.

He followed the Buick until it turned into the parking garage at the Hilton Hotel. By now it was getting lighter again and Jim had to be careful not to be detected. He parked the car on the street and looked into the open parking garage. He saw the man go to the lower-level elevator door of the hotel. Once the door closed, Jim ran to the elevator to see what floor it stopped on. It had stopped in the lobby on the first floor.

Jim took the elevator to the lobby hoping to rendezvous with Agent Youngblood. He wasn't sure if she'd had time to get there or not, but he hoped she had. As he entered the lobby, he immediately noticed the man in the Mariners hat standing at the counter. Jim quickly slid down the hallway so the man couldn't see him.

Just then, Jim's cell phone buzzed. The text was from Herman.

The text read, "Our man took the fiber optic node from the panel. Must intercept."

Jim was glad that he had asked Agent Youngblood to come. Now they would have to confront Mr. Mariner and that was better to do with support.

***

The man with the Mariners hat had been talking with the attendant at the front desk for a few minutes before she handed him a piece of paper. The man looked at the note and then went back to the elevator and pressed the button for the third floor.

Jim knew that the third floor of the Hilton were guest rooms. The man either had a room at the Hilton or he was meeting someone there.

The stairs were down the hall past Jim so he quickly entered the staircase so the man couldn't see him. He sent a text to Agent Youngblood telling her to go to the third floor and then he bolted up the stairs.

"Almost there." Read the text from Agent Youngblood, just as Jim hit the top of the second floor staircase.

Should he wait for her, or try to apprehend the man himself? Reaching the top of the third floor staircase, Jim carefully peered around the corner to see if the man was on the floor. He was just coming out of the elevator and then turned down the hall away from Jim. He knocked three times on room 317, the door opened quietly, and the man stepped inside.

"Good." Jim thought. "I can see who his contact is."

Jim watched for about five minutes when the elevator opened and Margie Youngblood stepped out. As she glanced down the hallway, Jim stepped out of the stairwell slightly, put his finger on his lips showing to be quiet, and waved her toward him. Agent Youngblood quickly joined him at the stairs.

"What's the plan here?" Agent Youngblood asked.

"The suspect is in room 317 meeting someone. He has a device on him that we must retrieve, but I'm hoping we can also find out who his contacts are."

"Okay. How about I continue to follow him and you apprehend whoever is in the room after he's gone?" Youngblood replied.

"I'm good with that." Jim answered just as the man came out of room 317 and walked toward the elevator. Agent Youngblood turned and started down the stairs, while Jim waited until the elevator door had closed.

***

Jim quietly walked to room 317, pulled his gun from the holster in the back of his jeans, and wrapped three times on the door. He ducked down so that whoever might look through the peep hole would not see his face.

"I told you not to come back here." A voice said as they opened the door.

Quickly Jim put his foot in the door and pushed his shoulder hard to open it further. The young Chinese woman on the other side of the door was startled and stepped backward.

Jim immediately pointed the gun at her and asked her for the fiber optic node.

"I don't know what you're talking about." The woman said.

"You do and I need it right now, or I'm going to splatter your brains all over this hotel room. Or maybe I'll just restrain you and let the Chinese have you." Jim said gruffly.

"Well, there's no need to get mean about it." The young woman said sarcastically as she kicked at Jim trying to dislodge his gun.

Jim was startled, but did not lose his grip on his weapon. He put his arm out straight and pushed the woman into a chair and then sat on her. With his free hand, he reached for his handcuffs and quickly cuffed the woman with her hands behind her back. He then made her stand before he had her lay face down on the floor.

As he patted her down to search for the node, he felt a small box shaped object in the woman's side blazer pocket.

"Thank you." He said as he pulled out the red node and slipped it in his pocket.

Jim took out his phone and sent a text to Agent Youngblood before he dialed Herman.

***

Yu Li knew what she was to say. She knew that claiming to be a tourist in a downtown Anchorage hotel would be the most believable scenario, but the agent had caught her with a delivery in her pocket. The "tourist" ruse would not work. Yu Li was devastated. She had failed and she and her mother would pay the price.

"My name Yu Li," she began in broken English…

Chapter 58

Kate and Emma both slept uneasily that night because of the strange encounter with the man in the Mariners hat and their dinner companions' strange behavior once Jim had seen him. Both women were happy with their decision to leave it all behind.

By 8:30am in the morning they had said good-bye to their host, Kevin, and were on the train headed for Whittier. Though this train did not have the windowed roof, it was a very comfortable train.

The three-hour ride passed quickly as they enjoyed the view and the company on the train. The train route slowly snaked eastward toward Whittier along the banks of the Turnagain Arm. The weather could not have been more perfect. The Northern Pacific was a bright blue with constant viewing of humpback and beluga whales, along with the typical shore birds such as black oystercatchers with their bright orange beaks, yellow-billed loons, and an occasional bald eagle.

The route also included steep mountains on the northern shore. The glacier valleys that seemed to thrust ice all the way to the train tracks, were ominous and overpowering the landscape.

After about two hours, the train slowed. Kate noticed that it seemed like there was a glacier right in front of them. It didn't look like the train could go any further, but she could not see a town anywhere.

Suddenly, cars began to drive by the train in the opposite direction. It seemed as though they were coming right out of the glacier in front of them. It was then that Kate realized that they must already be at the tunnel into Whittier. The tunnel opened to vehicles about every half hour. Once the vehicles have cleared the tunnel then the train could pass. The tunnel was only one lane so traffic could only pass through going in one direction so the rotation of cars and train was timed so that rail and auto could predict when the road was open in the direction needed. The train did have to wait about ten minutes before they could enter the tunnel.

The tunnel was an eerie experience. It was narrow, with only about a foot on either side of the train. As the train drew deeper into the tunnel, all sources of light were choked out and Kate and Emma could not see anything in the car or outside of it.

It seemed that the passage took about five minutes and then light shown again. The train opened up to an incredible scene. They were in a steep rugged sea inlet with many glacial peeks around them. Only in one direction did the view open up to the bay of Pacific water where they would soon meet the Alaska Marine Highway ferry, which would be their passage to Juneau.

The glaciers flowed nearly down to sea level in many places giving the impression of frozen rivers about to burst their dams.

Chapter 59

Jim's phone rang. He picked it up quickly.

"Jim, this is Youngblood. Our man got on the morning train to Whittier. I didn't think we should take him out until we knew where he was going. Once in Whittier, he seemed to be following two middle aged tourists. I'm not sure if they are accomplices or dupes, but they don't seem to know that he's there."

Youngblood continued, "He purchased a ticket on the Kennicott, which is leaving in an hour. I checked the schedule and it doesn't stop until Juneau in 3 days."

Jim was nervous. He knew that Kate and Emma had gone to Whittier this morning as well, and were scheduled to board the ferry to Juneau. "Tell me what the tourists look like." Jim asked.

"Women. One looks about 55, blondish gray and a little chubby. The other seems a little older, but smaller with white hair." Margie Youngblood reported. "Do you want me to get on the ferry? There's a lot of people and I think I could go unnoticed."

"Yes, and protect those tourists." Jim said as he hung up the phone.

Chapter 60

To the left of the train station in Whittier was a jagged mountain with a barely seen glacier on top where the melting waters flowed down in a magnificent waterfall into town. Whittier itself was merely one large apartment building and a few houses, with a large marina. The train station was located just out of the tunnel on the opposite side of the small gravel road from the marina. Kate and Emma, knowing that their ferry would not arrive for several hours, hoisted their backpacks and began walking into town.

"Let's find a place to store our packs and then get a bite to eat." Suggested Emma.

At the end of the marina there was a visitor's center with lockers big enough to store their packs. Once their load was lightened, they wandered around looking at the small village. One sidewalk led into the mountain and Kate realized that it was a tunnel. Exploring the tunnel, the women found that it went under the town and came out at the large apartment building nestled up by the cliffs of the mountain.

"This is curios," Emma said.

They decided to walk into the apartment building, thinking it odd that a large building such as this would be located here. Walking into the first floor of the building they found a small grocery store and post office boxes. Deciding to purchase a few snacks, Emma asked the clerk about the curious tunnel and apartment building. The clerk explained that most people in town lived in this single building, which is why the first floor was used for a store and post office. The tunnel was built because most people worked at the marina or near there and snow removal was complicated. So, instead of plowing the streets in the winter, the city decided to give everyone walking access to the marina area in a tunnel that could be used year-round.

The two women had a pleasant conversation with the clerk before heading back through the tunnel to the marina. The clerk had recommended that they eat at a little restaurant near the ferry dock, which Kate and Emma did. They spent the rest of their time in Whittier exploring the valley floor and watching the boats go in and out of the harbor.

That evening, the Alaskan ferry, The Kennicott, came into port. She was a beautiful ship, complete with overnight cabins, a galley, viewing decks, and a small movie theater. Kate and Emma had reserved a cabin because they would be on the ferry for three nights before reaching Juneau. There was not a bathroom in the cabin and it was not designed for travelers to spend much time in, but it did have bunk beds with a port hole and a locking door.

Chapter 61

He bought a dark rain coat at the Visitor's Center gift shop in Whittier so that he could disguise himself and avoid being noticed. Though his Chinese contact told him to never remove his Mariners hat until the mission was complete, the man put the hat in his coat pocket because he was sure the women would recognize it.

Once on the ferry, he found his cabin and locked himself in while he plotted how to get the phone. He may have to confront the women and prevent them somehow from telling anyone of his presence. He didn't want to neutralize them, but he was prepared to if necessary.

Confident that he would be able to get the sensor because the women could not leave the ship until they reached Juneau, he lay down in the white night and slept hard.

★★★

Agent Margie Youngblood was sure that neither the man in the Mariners hat nor the two tourists would recognize her from the train, but she kept her distance just in case. She watched as the man with the Mariners hat purchased and then put on a navy rain coat. He removed his hat and put it in his pocket. There must be a dozen or more people with a plain navy colored rain coat. She would have to watch closely in order to keep track of him.

Chapter 62

Herman met Jim at a one level brown house with a tapestry type garden squeezed onto the banks of Lake Hood. A turbo prop was tied to a small dock on the east side of the house. Jim could see Herman already on the dock, untying the plane.

"Get in." Herman instructed as he removed the ribbing and threw his bag into a compartment behind the cab, before sliding into the pilot's seat.

Jim quickly threw his bag in as well and latched the compartment before climbing in and pulling his harness tight.

"We should be able to arrive before the ferry gets to Juneau." Herman said. "We'll have to refuel in Yakutat, but I've radioed ahead and my friend will meet us there to speed up the process.

"That's good." Jim responded and then began to tell Herman what the results were of the interrogation of the young Chinese woman in the Hilton Hotel that he had apprehended. The woman claimed to be a tourist, but had just arrived in Alaska from Seattle on a work visa. She denied any connection with our man with the Mariners hat, but did let it slip that the node was worth a lot of money if she delivered it back home. She said she was a secretary and that she was not working for the Chinese. When Jim suggested calling the Chinese consulate in Seattle to corroborate her story, she changed her mind.

"She said she knew the man with the Mariners hat by the name of Ty." Jim continued, "She was contacted by a man named Mr. Wu in Shenzen to retrieve the 'little red box' from Ty. If she did, she would be paid 150,000 Yuan. If she didn't, then her mother in China would disappear. Of course, She took the deal. She didn't seem to have any idea what the node could do, and I think I believe that part."

"Okay. So, we have intercepted two of the sensors and kept a node out of Mr. Mariners hands... I mean, 'Ty.' But how do we know how many sensors are left and if he'll try for another node?" asked Herman

"I only know that Yu Li said she was expected to get two 'little red boxes' from Ty." Jim answered.

"I have a suspicion that Mr. Mariner has hidden sensors in Emma's phone. Otherwise, why would he have offered to take a picture for them and how did he manage to lock up the phone unless he slipped the case off and back on again?" Herman said. "We have to find Emma and Kate as soon as we get to Juneau. I'm worried we've let them walk right into trouble."

"Me too," Jim responded.

"Agent Youngblood is good at being invisible and she'll keep them safe." Herman reassured himself.

"Have you had any contact with Emma yet?" Jim asked.

"No, but they are still out at sea and I'm sure, without a satellite phone, I won't hear from her until at least tomorrow morning."

Chapter 63

Once they were settled with their things in their cabin, the women decided to explore the ship. They first went topside. It was a large ship. On the upper decks that were exposed to the weather, there was a covered area for those without cabins to set up tents that would not be subject to the rain, though it was open to the air so there was no wind protection.

Kate loved this! "I wish we'd have just done this with a tent."

"Not me!" Emma exclaimed. I don't sleep on the ground anymore. We can tell everyone we were roughing it, but I don't need to really do it."

Kate agreed with a chuckle. "It is getting cold and windy up here."

Moving around to the inside of the ship, there was an observation deck completely enclosed with comfortable reclining chairs. To the back of the room was a small movie theater. This was dark and had recliner chairs as well. When they walked in, a documentary on the history of gold mining in Alaska was playing. The women got a schedule for the cinema before they exited the room.

Next, they went to galley on the 5th deck. It was not large, but had everything one might need in order to make the three-day jaunt to Juneau, including sweatshirts and jackets for sale. The grill was off to the right and then snacks and other premade entrées were in windowed refrigerators that travelers could just grab, pay for, and go.

"Where's the coffee?" Emma asked, just as she spotted a large pot on the wall past the kitchen area. She walked to it and poured herself a cup.

They had departed Whittier just before the eight o'clock hour. At ten o'clock, night was still nowhere to be seen, so the two decided to bundle up and head for the upper deck again to see if they could spot some wild life.

Chapter 64

The first full day on the ship was fun for Kate and Emma. Though it was windy and cold, the sky was clear and the mountains to the east were breathtaking and never out of sight. They saw many humpback whales traveling with them along the coast of Alaska and once a large one even breached a couple of times just off of the starboard. Kate was so excited, because even though there was a man in a navy raincoat near the railing blocking some of the view, she was able to get pictures of it.

When the weather became too chilly, Kate and Emma would retreat into the observation deck lounge and sit in the recliners looking out the front windows of the ship. While the view of wildlife was not as good there, they found very interesting people to talk with.

One woman shared that she and her husband were camping at Harbor Side RV Park in their camper when the earthquake happened. The entire Kenai Peninsula was evacuated late in the night for fear of a tsunami. Kate and Emma empathized with her and shared their own story. The woman was so taken with Emma that she invited her to come and stay with her and her husband in Georgia should she ever travel that way.

"You are so kind." She told Emma. "Thank you for letting me just talk. I think I needed to."

Later in the day, Kate and Emma found their way to the movie theater to watch a documentary about the Hubbard Glacier and its glacial advancement in spite of climate change. It was very interesting to them since their ship currently was just off of Yakutat Bay where the Hubbard Glacier was located.

Emma had taken her phone so that she could take pictures. She put it in the seat next to her because it was bulky in her pocket. As the movie played, she heard the phone fall to the floor. She thought she saw movement in the chair, but when she looked behind her through the dark, no one seemed to be there. She then bent down, picked up her cell phone, and thought that it would be better if she just kept it in her jeans pocket.

***

He followed the women into the theater. It was dark in the room and he could easily slide into one of the chairs without anyone recognizing him. Looking around the room, he could make out several silhouettes of people, and found who he thought were the two women in the middle of the theater, one seat from the isle. As not to draw their attention, he sat quietly in the outside seat, one row behind them. When he did, he noticed that the woman with the targeted cell phone put it on the seat beside her. Now he could get what he needed without being detected. He silently and carefully reached his hand around the seat to feel for the phone.

As he touched the phone with his fingers, it slid off of the seat to the floor. He quickly pulled his hand back and stayed crouched down so he could not to be seen. When he felt that he could sit up, the woman had retrieved the cell phone and was putting it in her front pants pocket.

Chapter 65

The second full day on the ferry was just as breathtaking as the first as they sailed southward along the Alaskan coast. The unbelievable chain of snow-capped glacial mountains left Emma and Kate in awe. After every peak a glacier flowed down with large waterfalls or there was glacial calving at the base, falling into the sea. The view was so drawing to the women that they did not sleep much for fear of missing some of the scenery.

In addition, there was wildlife all around. There were humpback whales, a variety of shore birds, seals, and Dall's porpoise that followed the ship, either by riding on its wake of wind or water. The Dall's porpoise were of particular interest to Kate as they looked like miniature orca.

Kate and Emma retreated to their cabin about one o'clock in the morning to get a few hours of sleep before the ship docked in Juneau in the morning. Once they had everything ready for bed and both bunks securely in place, they walked down to the public bathroom at the end of the hall. Both women had used the facilities, washed their hands, and brushed their teeth. As Emma was finishing combing her hair, Kate stepped out of the bathroom and glanced down the hall toward their room. She saw a man in a navy rain coat trying to open their cabin door. Spooked, she quickly stepped back in the bathroom and used her body to prevent Emma from exiting.

"Stop," Kate whispered, as she put her finger over her mouth to signal Emma to be quiet.

"What is it?" Emma whispered.

"There is a man trying to get into our cabin." Kate answered. "I could be wrong, but I think it's the same man that was wearing the Mariners hat in Anchorage."

Emma, without pausing, stepped around Kate and slightly poked her head out of the bathroom door. The man was still there, in front of their cabin trying to pick the lock.

Emma quickly put her head back inside the door. "What should we do?"

Both women were silent a moment and then Emma suggested that they make a lot of noise so that the man knew that they were returning to their cabin. Maybe this would scare him off.

Both women began talking loudly. Kate opened the bathroom door and stood in it looking inside of the bathroom and not down the hallway so that the man would clearly see them.

The plan worked. As the women came out of the bathroom, the man was walking away from them down the corridor toward the opposite door. Kate and Emma quickly went to their cabin and locked the door.

"Oh my God!" Emma exclaimed. "He was clearly trying to get in our cabin."

"And I'm sure it was the same man that seemed to have followed us in Anchorage. But what does he want with us?" Kate added.

The women reviewed what had happened in Anchorage. Was he stalking them or was he looking for something that they had? They both had money and credit cards on them, but it was well hidden in their cash packs on their waist. Besides, every tourist in Alaska probably has money and a credit card...so why them?

"He did offer to take that picture?" Emma remembered.

"And he locked up your phone!" Kate gasped. "Did he look at your phone?"

"It doesn't usually lock up when you look at it...but," Emma paused, "It does lock up when you snap the case off."

Emma snapped off the cell phone case, put it on the bed, and examined the smooth phone. When she didn't notice anything different about the phone, she grabbed the phone case.

"What is this?" she said when she turned the it over.

"That's weird." Kate said. "What is it?"

The quarter-sized round metallic object was clearly out of place on the phone case. It looked similar to a lithium battery only thinner.

"I don't know, but it looks electronic. Is it a tracker?" Emma asked.

"I'm not sure, but if this guy is looking for that, your phone case is what he's after."

Emma reached for her makeup case and took out a pair of tweezers. She carefully pinched the side of the object and slipped the bottom of the tool slightly underneath it. With a steady pull she was able to remove it from the cell phone case. Holding it up with the tweezers she and Kate carefully inspected the object.

"Don't you think it's weird that once Jim and I spotted this guy at the restaurant in Anchorage, that Jim and Herman left abruptly. Now the man shows up again…where we are?" Kate questioned. "I don't think that's a coincidence."

"Yeah, something is not right with this whole situation." Emma agreed. "As soon as we port, let's get our rental car and get as far away from this ship as possible. I'm glad we didn't tell Jim and Herman where we were staying in Juneau."

"Me too." Kate echoed.

Emma emptied the drops of fluid from her plastic contact lens case and slid the object into it before putting it in her makeup case. Then the women propped both backpacks against the door, wedging them between the door and the lower bunk, keeping the door from opening even if the lock didn't work. With only a few hours before the ship arrived, neither woman wanted to sleep.

***

The man was frustrated that he was not able to get the last sensor. He would be delayed getting to the Auke Bay Communication Station if he didn't have the sensor when the ferry docked, his contacts would not be pleased.

He only had one more sensor to plant and one more node to retrieve. Why did this have to happen? He felt his emotions boiling inside him. He was ready to resort to drastic measures. He knew the docks well in

Juneau and knew of a perfect spot where he could take the phone by force and no one would see him or hear from the women again. Morning could not come soon enough.

Chapter 66

After a few hours, Emma sat up in bed and got Kate's attention.

"I have an idea," she said. "I don't need this stupid cell phone case anyway."

She popped her cell phone out of the case and held it up for Kate to see. "Do you have anything that's about this size?"

"Well, let's see." Kate began digging in her backpack. She pulled out a small booklet about the Alaskan mountains that she had collected at the Anchorage Chamber of Commerce building. "Will this work?"

Emma took the booklet and slid it into the cell phone case. The booklet was a little narrow for the case so Emma took it out and rolled a tissue up and placed it on the inside edge of the phone case. She then slid the booklet back into the case and it fit perfectly.

"I think I need to give this to that guy. Maybe it will keep him from following us." Emma explained.

"What are you going to do, walk right up to him and say, 'I think you're looking for this?'" Kate said sarcastically.

"No, but I am going to accidently leave it where he can easily find it." She said.

"Okay, once we get off of the ship, let's talk loudly about having to get something out of our backpacks. You put the phone somewhere visible, with just the backside of the case showing, and then we will leave it there." Kate brainstormed. "I don't want to wait around."

***

The man watched as the two women debarked the vessel. Just as they reached the end of the departure ramp, the chubby woman stopped and took her backpack off. The smaller woman put her phone on the ramp railing and did the same. Both women seemed to be looking for something then put their backpacks back on and walked away.

There was the phone in open view. If he was swift, he could grab it and slip away before anyone noticed. He was quick and soon the phone was safely in his pocket. He turned the opposite way of the two women and quickly jogged away.

Chapter 67

Kate and Emma wasted no time getting into the ferry terminal where the rental car counter was. Kate quickly finished the paperwork while Emma kept an eye out.

"You're so lucky to have gotten the last rental car we have." The car rental attendant said. "I hope you don't mind an electric car."

When the paperwork was done, they exited out the far door, and hopped into a small little blue electric car.

"Let's not go straight to the hotel in case the man follows us out of the parking lot. I'm going to just drive past the hotel so we can do a little sightseeing first." Kate said.

"Okay." Emma agreed.

Just as they were pulling out of the parking lot, Emma's phone dinged with a text message.

"It's from Herman," Emma shared.

He's wondering if we've made it to Juneau or not.

"Well, don't answer him." Kate ordered.

"I won't!" Emma responded.

Chapter 68

Agent Margie Youngblood watched the man in the navy jacket quickly take the cell phone from the railing and slide it into his pocket. She used her own phone to text as she reported the direction in which the man had gone.

"He's got the cell phone. He's coming your way. I'll text when I see what vehicle he's in." Agent Youngblood said into her phone.

"Got it. We'll intercept." The voice replied.

"I'll keep eyes on the tourists." She said, reassuringly, as she disconnected the call.

***

Agent Youngblood had not planned to be in Juneau so she had to think fast concerning transportation. The Auke Bay ferry dock was at least eight miles from downtown Juneau. She needed wheels.

The two tourists were at the rental car counter in the terminal. She would wait until they left and then rent a car.

"Sorry, I just gave out the last one." The rental car attendant replied once Agent Youngblood asked for a car, "but my brother rents his car privately. I can call him if you want."

Agent Youngblood thought about it for a minute, while she watched out the window, where the man with the Mariners hat walked to a motorcycle that was parked at the far end of the parking lot. "Do you have anything right here, right now?"

"Well, if you don't tell anyone, I'll give you my car for $1000 a day, but you'll have to also compensate me for the insurance and miles."

"Are you kidding me?" Youngblood responded.

"How bad do you want a car?" the attendant smiled slyly.

"Fine!" Youngblood responded, "but I think price gouging is very unethical."

She then texted, "Yamaha motorcycle, green tank, black helmet, navy jacket, jeans"

Chapter 69

Kate and Emma felt relieved to be driving on the 52-mile roadway going toward north Juneau. While Kate drove, Emma looked out the back window for some time before finally confirming that they were not being followed.

As the car moved up Glacier Avenue, Emma spotted their hotel along the roadway, pointing it out to Emma and making a note in her head as to where it was located.

"Where to first?" Emma asked.

"Well, there are obvious signs to Mendenhall Glacier, so let's go there first. It's a county park so there should be lots of people around."

Emma agreed and they made their way to the park.

The glacier glistened in the morning light. Emma and Kate were excited to see it along with the icebergs in the river in front of them. Walking along the sidewalk as they made their way to the bank of the river, there were swarms of Sockeye salmon swimming in the creek beside them.

"Can we stay here all day?" Kate asked with excitement.

They stayed in the park for about a half hour, before finally thinking that it was clear to make their way back to their hotel. Both women were tired and eager to get settled before doing more exploring.

Chapter 70

Once in downtown Juneau, the man parked his motorcycle in a side alley near the downtown area. The first cruise ships since the pandemic began had come into port and the streets were crowded. He slipped off his helmet, hooked it on the handlebars of the motorcycle, and put his Mariners cap back on. He slipped the cell phone case out of his pocket and immediately noticed that it didn't have the weight that he would have expected. With closer inspection he saw that there was no phone in the case, just a small booklet. Quickly taking it out of the case, his heart sank as he saw the sensor was not there.

Frustrated and angry he threw the cell phone case down, took his baseball hat off again, and reached for the helmet. He would not stay quiet nor invisible any longer. Those women would pay for duping him.

He knew, however, that when he got angry, he got sloppy. He took a big breath to calm himself. And then the thought came to him. The women obviously knew about the sensor. What if they were not innocent tourists? What if they were CIA all along and watching his every move? He must be careful.

***

Jim spotted the motorcycle long before it pulled into town. He slowly pulled his car in behind it, following at a distance. When the motorcycle pulled into an alley, Jim drove slowly past so he would not raise suspicion. The streets were crowded and there was no place to park. Jim turned right toward the Red Dog Saloon so that he could drive around the block. As he was just about to complete the block, the man on the motorcycle took off in a hurry back up Egan Drive. Not to look too obvious, Jim turned toward Egan Drive as well, steering right to follow.

He used one hand to dial his phone and put it on speaker.

"Not sure why, but our man just rushed back up Egan like a speed demon and headed north again." Jim said into the speaker.

"Okay. I'll keep an eye out. I have eyes on the tourists just leaving the glacier." Agent Youngblood responded.

"Maybe you should warn them." Jim suggested.

"I will if needed." She said, "but I think the less we involve them, the better."

Chapter 71

As he raced back up the two laned road, he watched the oncoming traffic to see if he could spot a rental car. Juneau was small and there were few rental cars. And, if you knew what to look for, they were pretty easy to spot. In Juneau, most of the electric cars are rentals. While there are a few personal vehicles that are electric, the only electric charging station is at the rental car lot at the Auke ferry dock, so most locals don't want to own one. Mendenhall Car Rentals, located right at the dock, has mostly electric cars in bright colors, so he assumed theirs would be easy to spot.

If they were tourists, they would go to the glacier first. That's where everyone wants to go. Not seeing any rental cars on the road between downtown and north Juneau, he turned toward the park.

***

Jim knew that he would be spotted if he tried to follow the man into the park. The road was narrow and there was no way for anyone to go past without being seen so he parked his car at the entrance in north Juneau before texting Agent Youngblood.

"Location?"

"Frontier Hotel" Agent Youngblood texted back. "blue electric rental, parked n back."

Jim then sent a text to Herman. "She is at Frontier Hotel."

Chapter 72

Not seeing any rental cars in the parking lot at the glacier, the man turned the motorcycle back toward north Juneau. He was glad he had fresh air blowing in his face because it was helping him to breathe deeply so he could control his building rage.

As he approached north Juneau he began cruising the side streets, slowly so that he could spot any rental cars. After searching for about an hour with no luck, he turned back southward toward town. There were several hotels between here and downtown. Maybe they were at one of those?

Chapter 73

Once at the motel, Kate suggested that they park the car around the back so that it would not be visible from the street. After checking into the hotel, they made their way to their room which was a large suite with a window on one end. The bedspreads were done with the Northwoods theme and there were paintings on the walls reflective of the area; one of a bear, one of an elk, and one of a moose.

"Where should I store this thing?" Emma asked holding up her contact lens case.

"I wouldn't put it anywhere in our things. Is there a drawer or a counter somewhere to hide it above or under?" Kate replied as both began looking about the room.

Between their queen beds there was a small table with a built-in lamp. The table was an octagon shape with a small wooden lip at the bottom. Emma felt to see if the lip was underneath the table as well. It was. She placed the single contact lens case on the lip inside and underneath the table.

"No one would see it or know where to look for it here if they didn't know." Emma said.

"I think we should take it to the local police today." Kate suggested.

"And tell them what? That we found this tracker but we have no idea who's it is or why we have it?" Emma questioned.

"You're right. That does make us sound dumb…and paranoid." Kate conceded.

After grabbing a snack, the two women went back to the car. They knew that Sheep Creek was the place to view the salmon run and that it should be really crowded this time of year. Having lots of people around gave them comfort and helped them make the decision on where to go while they decided what to do.

Chapter 74

Feeling an inevitable uncontrollable fury coming after failing to locate the two middle aged women, the man wandered further south toward downtown again. He had to apprehend them no matter what the cost. If he failed to plant the sensor this time, certainly it would be the end of him. But he didn't want to think of that now. He had to remain focused on retrieving the sensor and completing his mission.

Chapter 75

Emma's phone dinged with a text. "It's Herman again." Emma told her friend. "He says he is hoping we can talk."

"Ignore it." Kate said.

"I will for now, but maybe if I talked with him, he could explain what is going on." Emma said exasperated.

Both women were silent for a few moments as they drove south along Egan Drive toward Sheep Creek.

"Let's go to the salmon run and then decide what to do." Kate suggested.

"Yes," Emma replied. "There's nothing like some fresh air and a bit of nature to help you think clearly."

Downtown Juneau was about eight miles from north Juneau. It was crowded and a cruise ship was ported along the road on the right side. There was a busy parking lot with shops, and most notably, was a tram cable coming out of a building near where the cruise ship was moored. There were two cable cars that were in view; one going up and one going down.

Sheep Creek was not as far as Kate had thought. Only a few miles south of downtown, there was a large dirt pull-out on the road and a wide-open area with a creek running through it. There was only a small sign that said, "Sheep Creek," but it caught Kate's attention.

Kate parked the car and the women got out and went to the creek bank where a few people were jumping about and squealing with glee. As they neared the creek, Kate gasped as she noticed that the rocks that crossed the creek and took up the length of it, weren't rocks at all, but King salmon as far as the eye could see. There were dozens of seagulls diving into the biologically moving water and picking stuff off of the bank.

Both women became completely distracted and were mesmerized by nature's amazing circle of life. As they walked upstream, along the creek's bank, they came across piles of little orange salmon eggs that had been deposited. Some were dried out from the sun and others were being picked off by the squawking birds. Even with all of this commotion, there were many eggs that were in the creek near the edge that would renew the life of the salmon.

Walking up the creek, Kate and Emma were totally focused on the water, when Kate finally looked up to see how far they had come. When she did, she saw a black bear directly across the creek from them. The bear seemed to be ignoring them as he was feasting on the carcasses of dead salmon. The bear was so intent on eating, that it didn't seem to notice Kate and Emma. Kate tapped Emma on the shoulder and pointed toward the bear. She saw Emma's eyes light up and then Emma motioned that they should walk back down the creek. Kate followed.

As they walked back to the car, they talked with each other about the surprising experience and how amazing it was. Once back in the car Kate asked, "Is your mind clear now?"

"Totally!" Emma responded and she pressed her phone to call Herman.

Chapter 76

Herman was surprised when his cell phone rang. He picked it up without looking who was calling. "Hello."

"Hi, Herman."

He recognized her smooth voice immediately.

"Oh, wow! Thanks for calling me." He stammered. What was it with this woman? Why did she make him trip over his own words?

"Did you have something to say?" She asked sternly.

He hesitated. "Uh, what do you mean? I wanted to say hello."

"Cut the crap, Herman." She said curtly. "You have some questions to answer."

"I know. I know. Can you meet me in town? I hate to be cliche', but the Red Dog Saloon is easy to find and you can park at the cruise ferry lot across the street."

"You're in Juneau?" she asked.

He cursed himself for giving it away, but she would have figured it out soon anyway. "Yes."

"You do have some explaining to do." She said.

Once he hung up the phone he quickly jogged from where he was sitting near the library, to the Red Dog Saloon. Why had he suggested there? It would be crawling with people.

Chapter 77

He had spotted several rental cars going south on Egan, but none of them had the two women in them. However, just as he was turning left around downtown, he spotted a blue electric rental car parked at the ferry terminal that he had not seen before.

"They are downtown." He thought to himself.

He quickly pulled near the car and confirmed that it was a rental from Mendenhall Rental Cars. He then quickly scanned his eyes toward town. The streets were crowded with cruisers, but he thought he saw the smaller women walk into the Red Dog Saloon. Was it her? He wasn't sure but he was going to find out.

He quickly parked his motorcycle and jogged across the street.

Chapter 78

Herman spotted them a few seconds after getting to the saloon. He waited until they saw him and then waved them to him near the back of the room. He had been able to grab two chairs and a small cocktail table when he arrived and offered both women a seat.

"I think I'm fine standing." Emma said indignantly.

Just then a person in the table next to them said, "I'm leaving. You can have my chair."

Herman nodded thank you and pulled the chair up to the small table and sat down so that he had a view of the door. Kate and Emma then sat down in the two empty chairs.

"What would you like to know?" Herman asked innocently.

"Oh no." Kate responded. "Don't act stupid. We are being stalked by the same guy that you and Jim ran after in Anchorage. Why?"

Herman lowered his head as if to indicate the conversation should be private and then motioned with his hand for the women to move closer.

"And why did he put a tracker on us?" Emma asked.

"A tracker?" Herman asked.

"Yes, a tracker." Emma responded. "I found it in my cell phone case."

"Do you have it with you?"

"Not with me. I'm not stupid." Emma answered.

"Could you get it for me?" Herman pleaded.

"Not so fast." Kate piped in. "How do we know you're not the one who put it there? Look, you and Jim seem really nice, but we don't really know you. I think we should take it to the police."

"If you think that's what you want to do, please go ahead." Herman said.

Kate and Emma seemed surprised.

"You wouldn't mind if we did that?" Emma asked.

"Not at all." Herman said. "I just need it to be safe."

Just then Herman looked up. "You need to leave, NOW!" he said.

He stood up and the women stood as well.

"This way." He said as he put a hand on each of their backs and slightly pushed them toward the back door.

Confused, Kate looked back and saw the man with the Mariners hat. She ducked down and ran for the back door. Emma, noticing Kate's pace, followed. When they slipped out the back door and into the alley, they came face to face with a woman. Emma looked back for Herman, but he did not follow them.

"You need to follow me." The woman instructed.

Kate and Emma followed the woman across and down the alley and into the back door of a Harley Davidson shop. The shop appeared to be closed. The woman motioned them to a back room.

"Stay here and keep the door closed. I'll be back soon."

"Who are you?" asked Kate.

"My name is Agent Youngblood. I can't explain things right now, but I will soon. Please stay here where you'll be safe." She said as she left.

Chapter 79

Herman saw the man, and the man saw him turning from the back door. The man darted out of the front door and around the building into the alley.

"No." Herman thought and he jumped towards the back door in order to cut him off. As Herman went out into the alley he saw the man running at full speed. He had a gun in his hand and pointed it toward Herman.

"Where is my sensor?" he demanded.

"I don't know what you're talking about." Herman replied.

"Give it to me!"

"I don't have it." Herman shouted.

His temper was getting the best of him, he knew that, but he was tired and frustrated. "I want it now!"

"I told you, I don't have it." Herman repeated.

In anger the man stood at arm's length from Herman and put the gun on his forehead. "I said, Give it to me!"

Herman closed his eyes waiting for the shot, but it didn't come. When he opened his eyes, Agent Youngblood was standing to the man's right with her pistol pointed at the man's temple.

"Put it down." She said coldly.

"Herman quickly grabbed the short barrel of the man's Ruger and pointed it downward, then gripped the man's arm and turned him sideways with one hand behind his back. Youngblood kept her aim, barking instructions at the man. "Face down on the ground. Hands behind your back."

The man complied, waiting for an opportunity to escape.

Herman kneeled on the man's back and put cuffs on his wrists, just as Jim ran into the alley.

"A little late for the show." Herman joked to Jim. Then he looked at Agent Youngblood and said, "Thank you."

"No problem." Agent Youngblood responded.

Herman and Jim picked the man up, each holding one of his arms and escorted him into the back door of the Harley Davidson shop.

"There's no crowd in here." Agent Youngblood said.

Chapter 80

As Agent Youngblood was holding the door open for Herman and Jim to bring the man in, the man dove for her knocking her to the ground. He then darted toward the back of the shop toward the office.

As he knocked the door open, with hands behind his back, he was met with two faces. Instantly, something swung and hit him across the back and then another blow came to his forehead. The faces in front of him faded as he blacked out.

Herman and Jim ran to pursue the man, but once at the door, they saw him lying unconscious on the ground. Kate stood near the door with a Harley Davidson handle bar gripped firmly in her hands and Emma was shaking her fist and blowing on it.

"Ouch!" Emma said.

"Nice swing!" Kate cheered.

The men just stood there in bewilderment as Agent Youngblood came up behind them brushing the dirt off of her sleeve.

"Well, don't just stand there. Get him out of here." She told them.

★★★

Within minutes two patrol cars and four deputies were at the Harley Davidson shop in response. The man, Ty Remini, was hauled to one of the police cars, still half dazed.

"Thank you." Herman said. "We owe you both an explanation."

"Yes, you do." Emma said. "So, let's have it."

Herman and Jim together explained about the Chinese spy ring attempting to access classified weaponry using sensors like the one Emma had. They admitted that they were not brothers, but colleagues, along with Agent Youngblood, and that they had been following Remini all along.

"So, you used us?" Emma said.

"I know it looks that way, but we didn't try to and I really do think you are wonderful." Herman responded.

Emma smiled.

Kate smiled at Emma. That was the Emma she loved. The one who could stand up for herself and yet find the good in everyone.

"Do you feel confident enough to get the sensor for me now?" Herman asked Emma. "You can give it to the police if that makes you more comfortable."

"How about both." Emma said, as she flagged down an officer to take her and Herman back to the Frontier Hotel to retrieve the sensor.

"I'll meet you there, Emma." Kate said, "I'll have to get the rental car."

"May I ride with you, Kate?" Jim asked.

Kate thought for a moment, and then simply said, "Sure."

Chapter 81

Jim and Herman arrived at Clear early the next morning after making sure that Ty Remini was securely in custody. Because he had been deemed a threat to national security, Remini would be kept in a top security facility until they could convince him to share more information concerning his contacts in China and elsewhere.

The Chinese spy network had grown and were becoming more aggressive even though it felt to Jim like he was often chasing ghosts. Finally, Remini could be the link they needed.

The two men knew that their work was just beginning. However, they were both relieved that Remini had been apprehended without injuries or loss of life. They knew that Remini was capable of harming others and felt fortunate that everyone, especially Kate and Emma, were safe.

***

Jim contemplated his future. He was 64 years old and getting too old to chase men half his age around the wilderness of the north.

Herman was two years older and was feeling his age. Both had had honorable careers and talked about retirement. In their field they had been given assignments around the world. They had worked with all nationalities of people from many different cultures. And when it had been called for, they were assigned to survive alone in the wilds of the planet for weeks without human contact. Though they had many years where they worked with other agents, both preferred working with each other.

Now, however, maybe it was time to ride off into the sunset.

Chapter 82

As they sat down to Thanksgiving dinner, Emma noticed that Kate was preoccupied with a text message on her phone. Trying to distract her friend, she said, "Last summer's journey through the white night was such an adventure. It was scary, but so amazing."

"I don't ever want to go through that again." Kate retorted.

Kate took out another plate with utensils and put it on the table next to Emma before she laid her own plate down.

"I'm going to wait a minute to eat if that's okay with you, Emm."

"Of course." Emma responded. "Are you okay?"

"Yes, but I just want to get some air first." Kate told her.

"Okay, I'll go with you." Emma said with concern.

As Emma opened the door, staring at her with his lovely deep brown eyes, was Herman. Emma was speechless.

"I thought that since you were something that I was really thankful for, I'd join you for dinner." Herman said pulling a bouquet of flowers from behind his back.

Emma gasped and then her squeals could be heard down the block. She jumped up and hugged Herman before planting a juicy kiss on his lips.

"I guess that means, yes." Herman laughed.

Kate could only smile. She and Herman had been planning this meeting for a few weeks because she knew that Emma had talked of nothing except him since they left Alaska. Emma deserved to be happy and Herman was a standup guy.

As Emma escorted Herman into her house, Danish rushed out the door barking.

"Danish!" Kate scolded.

When she looked up to see what the dog was barking at, there was Jim coming down the driveway.

"I hope you don't mind that I tagged along." He grinned. "Herman and Emma shouldn't have all the fun."

Kate smiled.

About the Author

Dana Chandler has been an educator for most of her career, as a teacher and a school principal, in the United States and abroad. She was raised in a large family who loved to tell stories. She published her first book after her experiences in Japan during the 2011 earthquake and tsunami. It was then she realized that she wanted to continue writing.

Other published works by Chandler include:

1. *Lil* (Co-authored by Kari Lineberry)

2. *When the World Shakes: A Personal Account of the 2011 Great Tohoku Earthquake and Tsunami*

3. *Hello! I Have Autism*

Chandler has also written and published curricula and self-study books for educational purposes.

Lil

(Excerpt from the novel)

The year was 1919.

"Help! Help! Mama, please help!" Mary Anne heard the scream from 11-year-old Lil. She turned and ran to the back of the house where Lil was attempting to hold John up. John was white as a sheet and seemed semi-conscious. Mary Anne helped Lil lay him down on the floor where she quickly went to work assessing what was wrong with him.

"Did your brother fall, Lil?"

"No, Mama. He said dinner had upset his stomach, and he wasn't feeling so good and then started to collapse. I tried to catch him but he's too big." A tear ran down her cheek.

"*Dobrý, Lil. Dobrý.*" Mary Anne tried to reassure her and then called the older boys in from their evening chores to help her get John into bed. Mary Anne busied herself boiling water for sanitizing the house with lye. Bill and Harry obediently told a bedtime story to Irene, and Larry and put them to bed. George took care of Little Teddy so Mary Anne could do the cleaning and give orders for John's care. Emotions were high, but the children did what they were supposed to.

A cold wind started to blow during the night, so Frank and the older boys kept the wood stoked in the stove to keep the house warm. Within hours, John was sweating profusely and had spiked a fever. He was seeing things and talking in gibberish and had started to cough. Mary Anne instructed Emily to keep rags soaked in cool water on his head in an attempt to bring the fever down.

In the meantime, Mary Anne showed Lil how to make her grandmother's famous purple willow bark tea. "It's a miracle medicine." She was calm, but calculated, as she measured the dried and ground bark from the jar. Lil helped her boil the water and measure. "You will need to know this someday for yourself, Lil. It will kill a fever and loosen the chest. Good thing we have the river to keep the willows moist in the summer. It makes for better bark tea."

By early morning, John was continuously coughing, and his chest was heaving up and down as he labored for each breath. Mary Anne held John's hand most of the night and sang sweet songs in his ear. He was no longer talking, and his skin color had turned slightly blue-ish yellow. It was apparent that he was suffering seriously and that it was time to fetch a doctor.

There wasn't much sleeping that night for Mary Anne and the older children. They were all worried about John. Mary Anne gathered the older children together and said a quick prayer. She wasn't much good at praying but thought it couldn't hurt. As she said a quick, "Amen," she heard Irene crying from her bed.

"I don't feel good Mama."

Mary Anne felt her head. She was hot and very pale. "Oh, no. It's contagious," she thought to herself. "Emily, fetch another rag for Irene. And Lil, make sure she gets some tea too!"

And with that, she picked Irene's three-year-old body up, wrapped her in a blanket, and laid her on the floor next to John. At least she would try to confine the sick ones to one area of the house. "Emily, you keep cold rags on their heads. Lil, keep giving them sips of the tea. Everyone else keep your distance for now. We don't know what this is that's making them sick, and I sure don't want anyone else catching it."

Emily and Lil did what they were told.

At daybreak the snow started falling, and Frank knew he would have to go to town, even with the horrible weather. He bundled up as quickly as he could, fixed their only good wool blanket over his shoulders, and ran as fast as he could through the snow toward town.

Mary Anne boiled more water for cleaning and hand washing. Joseph and George brought buckets of snow inside by the fire and let it melt slightly so Emily would have ice cold water for treatment while Joseph snuggled newborn Teddy to keep him happy. Junior made a few trips to the barn to fetch milk for the children and to feed Baby Teddy so Mary Anne could tend to John and Irene and continue sanitizing the house. The little ones, Bill, Harry, and Larry played quietly in one corner. The two boys, Bill at seven and Harry at five, were masters at keeping the toddler occupied.

It was three hours later when Frank returned home. He was cold and snow covered. "*Kde je* doctor?" Mary Anne quickly asked. "Someone get your Papa some water!"

"The doctor is busy, Mary Anne. Half the town is sick like John. He says it's a strange flu, and it's highly contagious. Some in town are saying that it hit parts of the west last year, but this year it's worse. The doctor isn't making it, Mary Anne. We're on our own. I know you think others can pray better than you, but you can pray better than you think. I suggest you do it."

"Irene's sick too, Frank. Are we all going to get sick?" Mary Anne's voice broke.

"Now, Mary Anne. Let's not be thinking that way. We will get through this. They told me in town that the doctor is telling everyone to take something called As-parn every day, but there isn't any left in town.

You don't suppose that miracle tea you make would do the same thing, do you, Mary Anne?"

"What is that?" Joseph piped in.

"It's called aspirin," Mary Anne corrected. "And yes, the willow bark tea will do the same thing. We are good then." She went back to the stove and poured more water from a bucket into a kettle for making more tea. "Lil, *pojďme na to*!"

"Your Mama is better than a doctor!" With that, Frank unwrapped his coat. He was dripping with sweat himself and was tired. "I'm going to lay down for a bit."

As the day passed, John grew worse. By evening, he was in dire condition. He hadn't eaten and had stopped drinking, so Lil started dipping a small cloth in the tea and gently ringing it out near his lips hoping he would draw the moisture from it into his mouth. "That seems to be helping." Her words came out quietly. John just groaned.

Mary Anne went to wake up Frank, who had been sleeping since he returned from town. Frank stood up and then collapsed on the floor beside the bed. "Joseph!" she shouted with a panic. "Come help me with your father!" Frank too had fallen victim to the sickness and had a high fever.

Sometime in the middle of the second night, Emily got sick, then Harry, then George. By the end of the second day, Joseph and Larry had symptoms along with Lil and Baby Teddy. Mary Anne had lined up sheets on the floor for each family member to sleep on, but they were short on blankets. She and Junior kept the fire stoked and used coats and winter clothing to cover the smaller children.

The situation seemed hopeless. All of the "what-if" scenarios that played out in Mary Anne's head were maddening. She had a bad feeling in the pit of her stomach. She didn't know how to do it properly but, after gathering her rosery beads, she prayed for some kind of supernatural intervention on her family's behalf. "Please God. If you're really there, make them better." It came out as a whisper under her breath.

Mysteriously, Junior did not have any symptoms, so he helped Mary Anne. He worked very hard taking care of everyone else. He was exhausted but otherwise healthy.

By the third night, even Mary Anne felt achy. She pushed back the symptoms and told herself that she was just tired, but by midnight, she couldn't deny it any longer. "Junior, I've got it too. I've got to lay down."

Junior had a frightened look on his face. "I'll take care of you Mama."

And he did. He became like a war hero on the front lines that day. Junior carried water, hauled wood for the fire, tried to keep Teddy fed, and cleaned up the vomiting messes that went along with the illness, all while tending to that precious miracle tea that Mary Anne had made and giving each person in the house a cup before bed. Lil admired his steadfastness and compassion as he took care of everyone. She gained a great respect for him during this time of her life.

By daylight on the fourth day, Lil already felt better. She could tell she still had a bit of a fever but was in good enough shape to help Junior with the chores and medicinal tea regiment.

On the afternoon of the seventh day, John opened his eyes, took a deep breath, sat up, and declared very loudly, "I'm hungry, Lil! What's for breakfast?"

Lil laughed out loud. "Anything you want Brother, anything you want!" After a week that seemed like a year, she finally felt hope rise in her heart.